HOMEOPATHIC MEDICINE

HOMEOPATHIC MEDICINE

A Doctor's Guide to Remedies
for Common Ailments ∎

TREVOR SMITH, M.D.

HEALING ARTS PRESS
Rochester, Vermont

Healing Arts Press
One Park Street
Rochester, Vermont 05767

Library of Congress Cataloging-in-Publication Data

Smith, Trevor, 1934-
    Homeopathic medicine : a doctor's guide to remedies for common ailments / Trevor Smith.
        p.   cm.
    Includes index.
    ISBN 0-89281-293-1
    1. Homeopathy.   I. Title.
RX71.S53   1989
615.5'32--dc20   89-7525
                                                                                  CIP

Printed and bound in the United States

10 9 8 7 6 5 4 3 2 1

Healing Arts Press is a division of Inner Traditions
International, Ltd.

Distributed to the book trade in the United States by Harper and
        Row Publishers, Inc.
Distributed to the book trade in Canada by Book Center, Inc.,
        Montreal, Quebec
Distributed to the health food trade in Canada by Alive Books,
        Toronto and Vancouver

CONTENTS

Cogito, ergo sum.
(I think, therefore I am.)

Descartes

PREFACE

This very simple and practical guide book to basic homoeopathy is written for the family by a practising general physician, to provide a readily available reference to the main treatments recommended for the common ailments and first-aid problems occuring in the home.

The book is divided into five distinct sections dealing with (1) the common problems and mishaps of childhood; (2) the awkward emotional problems of the adolescent; (3) the sudden, unexpected acute illnesses of the adult couple; (4) the challenge of middle age and the problems it may bring; (5) the elderly and the special difficulties involved in caring for them. In each section there is a general note which is psychologically oriented to help towards a more understanding approach to the delicate emotional problems which occur in every age. This is followed by a detailed listing of the common physical illnesses in each group, and how best to treat them homoeopathically, with a guide to the most appropriate remedies.

As with homoeopathy generally, the aim is to place equal emphasis on both the mental and physical aspects of health. The importance of an open-minded general approach and attitude to all illness, whatever its form, whether physical or emotional, is underlined.

Finally, this is essentially a very practical everyday book, to be used as a ready source of reference. It is recommended that it be kept easily available along with your treatment record sheets so that all the illnesses and the details of their treatments with the results, can be conveniently recorded. This is important in the event of a similar problem occuring in the same member of the family at a later date.

It is a book to be added to in terms of further experience with new and additional treatments, and is, above all, a book to refer to, to write in, and to use.

HOW TO USE THIS BOOK

1. Decide the nature of the problem and refer to the index to find the treatment giving details of recommended remedies.

2. Using the main symptoms (or complaints of the patient), and also the signs (anything abnormal that you observe), find the remedy which most closely fits the illness picture that you observe, and the patient complains of.

3. When the symptoms are those of a well-defined and clearly physical problem — e.g. a fall, burn, grazed limb, ear ache or throat infection — give the remedy recommended in the sixth potency (or strength) three times daily.

4. If there is no response to the sixth potency treatment after twenty-four hours, consult the relevant page again, and give the next nearest remedy which corresponds to the symptoms of the illness in the same potency three times daily.

5. If, having given a second remedy in the sixth potency, which seems well indicated from the notes, the patient is no better, then give the remedy which you first chose (the one that matches the symptoms best) in the thirtieth potency every hour for six doses, or until there is an improvement response. If there is no response after the hourly use of the thirtieth potency, or the patient is getting worse, and the condition gives cause for alarm, you should consult your doctor immediately.

6. When there are marked mental and psychological disturbances, give the remedy which most closely fits the symptoms in the thirtieth strength three times weekly only. Such emotional disturbances may be

present alone, or sometimes be linked to the typical associated physical problems listed. For example, bouts of tantrums and rage together with teething problems (*Chamomilla*), or an adolescent depressive problem with marked irritability, constipation and gastric problems (*Nux Vomica*).

7. When there is a psychological problem, whatever the age, refer to the general section of the particular age group for help with the best and most sensitive approach to such difficulties. Only then refer to the index and the reference sheets for the recommended remedy.

8. When there is a problem of severe collapse, high fever, vomiting, the absence of flatus (or gas) passed from the bowel, or the abdomen feels hard, or there are complaints of severe unbearable pain, or the pulse is weak, you should call your doctor for advice, and not attempt to treat the problem yourself.

9. Having diagnosed the condition and selected the remedy, make an immediate note of the following points, using a record sheet drawn up as on page 11. This might best be done using an exercise book which can be kept with this book.

   (a) The name of the person, age, and date.
   (b) The main symptoms with a note of any modalities (aggravating factors).
   (c) The exact time of the onset of the symptoms.
   (d) The remedy used, its strength or potency, and the frequency given.
   (e) The outcome of the treatment, how soon there was a response to the remedy, and in the case of an absence of response, this should also be noted.

10. With the higher potencies of 30c and above, a single dose may effect a considerable improvement and sometimes a complete cure. As soon as an improvement occurs it is usually unnecessary to give further doses of the remedy. When there is apparent relief, but the initial symptoms occur again, continue the same treatment until relief is maintained.

   If, after an apparent improvement, symptoms return, but in slightly changed pattern, select a new remedy which best fits the changed illness picture. Give this new remedy in the same strength and frequency as before until improvement is satisfactory.

   Note that the sixth potency is much more directed at local conditions, and it is much more unusual for the single dosage at this strength to effect such rapid results.

Example of Family Record Sheet

Date and Time of onset	Name	Main Symptoms	Modalities (aggravating factors)	Remedy used and potency	Outcome of Treatment

**Twenty Basic Homoeopathic Remedies for the Family
Medical Chest**

1. *Aconitum*	6. *Carbo Veg.*	11. *Kali. Bich.*	16. *Nux Vomica*
2. *Arnica*	7. *Chamomilla*	12. *Ledum*	17. *Phosphorus*
3. *Arsenicum Alb.*	8. *Gelsemium*	13. *Lycopodium*	18. *Sepia*
4. *Belladonna*	9. *Hepar Sulph.*	14. *Mag. Phos.*	19. *Sulphur*
5. *Bryonia*	10. *Hypericum*	15. *Natrum Mur.*	20. *Thuja*

Ointments: One tube each of Calendula and Hypercal.

The above should be purchased from a reputable homoeopathic chemist. With the exception of *Chamomilla*, which should be ordered in the granular form, the remedies should be bought as tablets in the 6th and 30th centesimal potency. The 7 gram size of tube is adequate for most families, and the list can be added to with experience. The remedies should be stored in an air-tight, clean box in a dry, cool and dark place, away from any strong smells such as camphor or perfumes.

If, at any time, a remedy has been given and the response is unsatisfactory, despite the fact that the clinical picture (or symptoms of the patient) seems to strongly indicate that particular remedy, then it is wise to buy a new supply and to dispose of the tablets you had in stock.

There is no danger of harm occuring from an excessive dose of the tablets, and even if they were taken in toto the worst effects might be a mild stomach upset. Nevertheless, they should always be stored in a safe place, away from inquisitive children, and quickly available when needed. Remember to always take the family homoeopathic remedies with you when going on holiday as it is often during such times that they are needed most.

INTRODUCTION

Homoeopathy was founded as a viable alternative to conventional medical methods by the German physician Samuel Hahnemann at the beginning of the last century. Increasingly concerned about the dangers and complications of the crude physical methods common in the treatments of his day, he evolved a more gentle and effective approach based on ancient principles of healing. Despite enormous opposition, he very effectively used natural substances of plant, animal and mineral origin which had the properties of stimulating the body's curative response to disease. Beginning with his classical proving experiments with Quinine bark used in the treatment of malaria, he eventually was able to develop a wide range of healing substances, after many years of research, which now form the basis of the modern homoeopathic pharmacopoeia. The approach has stood the test of time, and there is now an increasing number of clinics and treatment centres using his methods, in many parts of the world.

Both in substance and action the remedies used in homoeopathic prescribing differ totally from most of the drugs used in conventional medicine today. Although treatments have become more sophisticated since Hahnemann's time, in many ways, orthodox attitudes and approach to the patient have remained much the same. There is still the same tendency for excessive, heavy-handed treatments with prolonged over-prescribing, which is rarely justified. At the same time, the use of suppressant drugs with the sole aim of eradicating symptoms, can leave the patient just as exhausted and weak as the earlier historical treatments of blood-letting and purgation. In addition there are often added complications of undesirable side-effects, and frequently severe problems of addiction and dependency. Once the umbrella effect of such palliative measures wears off, there is frequently the re-emergence of a more severe and uncontrollable form of the original problem, making subsequent treatments more prolonged and complicated.

The homoeopathic principle is perhaps best summed up by the Latin phrase *similia, similibus, curentur,* meaning: 'let like substances be used to treat like diseases'. The Greek word 'homoeopathy' means 'equal or similar illness', and refers to the unique homoeopathic principle of using the 'like' or 'similimum' remedy to effect a cure. The similimum remedy is that substance which when given in its natural undiluted form stimulates a pattern of symptoms which are similar to, but naturally not identical to those of the original illness.

In order to understand the similimum principle, it is useful to look at some well known examples of homoeopathic principles at work. *Belladonna,* taken in its natural form of the common hedgerow poison Deadly Nightshade, provokes a high restless fever, thirst, irritability, a hot burning skin, and a burning sore throat and ear. *Belladonna* taken in its homoeopathic form is curative for the child with similar symptoms, who is restless, has a high fever, is thirsty, burning hot, irritable, with an acute inflammatory sore throat or ear infection.

In the same way, vinegar, or acetic acid, applied to the skin in its concentrated form is often an irritant, causing redness, irritation, and intolerable itching. It is also a well-known household remedy for insect bites, and gives rapid relief particularly to the bites of the red ant family, which attack by injecting minute amounts of the related formic acid into the skin, causing burning redness, irritation, and itching. In this way, vinegar is being used homoeopathically, and according to similimum principles, although it has not on this occasion been converted into its more diluted remedial form.

The homoeopathic remedies are prepared in serial dilutions of the natural substances which have been found by clinical experience to stimulate a curative action. The dilution of the remedies to infinite proportions, during their preparation, is one of the unique features of homoeopathy, and is a safeguard against toxicity and side-effects of the treatment. At the same time, this dilution of the remedies adds to their power to stimulate a response. Such principles are now quite familiar in nuclear physics and in modern energy theories. With increasing technology and advances in the analysis of blood and serum chemistry, especially the use of the electron microscope, trace elements have been found to play a significant role in health, although present in the body in much the same scale of dilution as is used in homoeopathy. A further feature in the preparation of remedies is that, during the essential process of dilution, each successive potency or dilution is strongly agitated, or vitalized, by vigorous shaking. This develops the special properties of the remedy. It is, naturally, a time-consuming process and demands great attention to accuracy and purity.

The potencies and strength of a remedy relate directly to the degree of serial dilution, that is, the higher the dilution of the mother tincture the greater the power of the remedy to act. As a remedy is diluted — for example, using the centesimal scale common in the U.K., to the 6th potency (10^{-12}) or to the 30th potency (10^{-60}) — its breadth and scope of action is intensified. At the 6th potency the remedy acts much more at a tissue or pathological level — I like to think of this as acting at a functional level — whilst when the 30th potency is used the psychological sphere as well as the tissues is included in the remedy's range of action.

Homoeopathy does not claim to be a panacea or cure-all, nor a complete substitute for all the advances of modern medicine and surgery. However, for many conditions it offers a safe and rapid alternative to drugs, many of which are ineffective and potentially harmful. For example, recent research has shown that colourants in the coatings of certain drugs used in the treatment of asthma can produce an allergic response, provoking the very spasm and problems which they claim to cure.

A further unique feature, is the attention a homoeopathic practitioner pays to his patient and to the very many personal factors that contribute to his level of health or sickness. Both the emotional as well as the physical aspects of the person are used, side by side, to form an overall picture as a basis for diagnosis and prescribing. The degree of development and maturity, together with the many variables or modalities of response to food, weather, noise, and other people, are all considered. Finally a remedy is decided upon that not only fits the particular symptoms, but also the unique individual, his or her life style and pattern of health and illness.

In recent years, more families than ever have sought in homoeopathy an alternative to conventional medicine. There are many reasons for this change of outlook which is world-wide and expresses a profound dissatisfaction with an approach which is over-mechanical and based on the suppression of symptoms. Such suppression, of course, leads ultimately to the suppression of the individual, rather than a concern for his growth and development, and an understanding of his illness and its overall meaning.

In general, people are becoming increasingly thoughtful and discriminating. They want to be better informed by their doctors of the risks involved in their treatments and may want to consider an alternative choice. At best, patients need more of a say and a discussion in what substances are used to treat them, their families, and their children in order to understand more fully the implications and complications of such treatments. It is also true that more and more people now accept that they have a responsibility, not only for the quality of their lives generally, but also for the degree and quality of their health.

When considering the common problems which occur in the home and family, it is, first of all, important to understand what we mean by health, in order to come to a better understanding of the lack of it in illness and disease. Health certainly implies a feeling of well-being in the psychological sense as much as in the physical. There must be not only a freedom from physical pain and discomfort, but a general sense of harmony, with an absence of mental anxiety, tension and fear. Short-lived, transient symptoms are the price we all pay for living in a jet-age society, and these reflect environmental pressures especially those of noise and pollution. For many, over-crowding, with poor working and living conditions are an added burden. All of these take their toll of the organism, often imperceptibly at first.

Normally, in health, there is a pleasant awareness of the body — a sense of the heart beating without palpitations, of the body moving and the lungs breathing — with a general feeling of enjoyment in whatever activity the body is engaged in. This subtle sense of health is impaired in the very early stages of sickness and there follows the vague, off-colour feelings of irritability, fatigue and lassitude which are common at the beginning of illness. It is important to realize that stress, or damage, can occur at several quite distinct levels, depending upon the severity of the stress, the resistance of the particular individual, and his general fitness and health.

Common Types of Stress Which Cause Illness

At a physical level, damage may be caused by the commonplace traumatic happenings at home or school, as with a cut, fall or bruise, or perhaps sudden exposure to damp cold or a biting east wind. Excess heat can also cause stress, provoking collapse and coma.

Where stress is at a deeper psychological level, the effects may be more damaging and long lasting. This may occur when there has been the sudden loss of a close friend or relative, or during the break-up of a marriage or relationship, or through severe difficulties at work or school. In situations where people have been victims of an actual physical assault, the emotional shock may take far longer to heal than the external physical injury.

There is stress at a chromosomal or inherited level. Here there is a familial or hereditary tendency to weakness in a certain organ or part of the body which may have occured over several generations. These factors are often present in diseases such as migraine, asthma, heart disease, blood pressure, eczema, and some of the rare diseases such as haemophilia. These hereditary factors which cause an increased disposition to specific diseases are called miasms. Hahnemann considered that they were passed on from one generation to another and were an important cause of chronic illness and various incurable health problems. Because of the weakness they engender, they are an underlying stress factor, and may encourage the demand for repeated prescriptions of sedatives and tranquillizers in a futile endeavour to relieve symptoms that are recurrent and do not respond to conventional treatments.

The deepest level is not easily definable, and is best called 'existential' or spiritual stress. It is very common in our present society, and is similar to, yet quite distinct from, emotional illness. Although anxiety and anguish commonly accompany it, the problem lies much deeper, and is characterized by loneliness, confusion about role and identity, and doubts about the purpose, and meaning of life. There is usually an associated depression and sadness, but this is at a surface level only and is a complication of the deeper crisis where aims, beliefs, faith and the whole reason for living and man's very existence is brought into question.

Basic to homoeopathic thinking, and a fundamental concept of treatment and cure, is that symptoms change during the course of treatment. Such changes follow well-defined principles which were first advanced by the American homoeopath Constantine Hering at the end of the last century. Hering observed that the original presenting complaints often tended to change position, or to shift from the upper part of the body to lower areas as a response to treatment. For example, a skin rash may move from the scalp to the shoulders; or an arthritic pain change from the neck region down to the hands. The symptoms also shift from the deeper and more vital organs to less vital and more superficial ones. The pain of angina may be relieved, only to be replaced after a short period by rheumatic discomfort in the hands or feet, the change being from an illness of the more central cardiac system of the body to the more peripheral and relatively less important joint and articular areas.

It is also fundamental to homoeopathy that the most recent symptoms are relieved first, and then are often replaced by others which date from an earlier period. These may be recurrent, or even forgotten problems, often having been partially suppressed by ineffective conventional treatments over the years and never fully cured or relieved. Such earlier symptoms, having reappeared, can now be more effectively dealt with by the homoeopathic remedy.

Hahnemann emphasized that homoeopathy can only be fully effective provided that there is no underlying mechanical or obstructive cause for the symptoms and illness. For example, when there is a displacement of the spinal column, or an obstruction of the bowel, perhaps due to scar tissue or fibrosis, the mechanical blockage must be relieved by manipulation or surgery before homoeopathy can be curative. When the problem is less severe, such remedies as *Graphites*, or *Thiosinaminum* can be very effective in breaking down the adhesions and scar tissue. Prior to surgical or physical intervention, the homoeopathic remedy can be of value in reducing the side-effects of the operation and keeping discomfort to a minimum.

From the beginning Hahnemann stressed the importance of the mind in health, and he held that it is the quality of our attitudes and thinking which gives the key to our basic resistance and vitality. There is no artificial separation of mind and body; and homoeopathy gives as much significance to the mental processes of the person as to the physical, in determining the underlying cause of illness and its treatments. There is always an underlying, often hidden and unexpressed, emotional element. This concept was expanded by such eminent physicians as Freud and Groddeck almost one hundred years after Hahnemann laid the foundations of homoeopathy firmly in the psychology of the individual. Changes in the mental state commonly precede the development of bodily symptoms as the healing energy forces attempt to eradicate them. The homoeopath sees disease as a state of sickness of the whole person and not just as some isolated happening in a joint or limb, unrelated to attitudes and feelings.

Most of the trivial day-to-day mishaps in the home, apparently caused by carelessness, fatigue and inattention, are often warning signals of deeper emotional problems breaking through the surface. Many of the common-place symptoms that trouble us, such as migraines, indigestion, skin problems, car accidents, or the flare-up of an old ulcer problem, are usually only the outer manifestation of underlying tensions. Families with young children, especially when there is a sensitive child, are usually well aware of this. Such problems as anxiety about a change of school, a coming examination, or an upset friendship, are recognized as significant factors preceding the development of a physical complaint or illness. Eczema, asthma, sore throat, grumbling appendix, and tummy upsets are some of the more common childhood illnesses which often have a psychological background.

Society and the world in general is in an ever-changing state of flux and movement, particularly in the area of personal values, morals and ethics. Ideals and codes of behaviour are changing and evolving at an ever-increasing pace. These external changes in society reflect changes occuring within the family unit as well as pressures upon it. Difficulties are therefore created for many families when these changes are too rapid for adjustment to occur, so that pressures and misunderstandings easily develop. Often it is this combination of accelerating social change and struggles in the family which causes illness and breakdown.

Homoeopathy has a great contribution to make to some of the problems of our increasingly mechanical and pressurized society by its broad approach to the whole person; and its ability, in the highest potencies, to open up the imaginative aspects of the mind and personality. This can often lead to an easing of many of the blocks in understanding, attitude and perception, which so often lead to sickness and ill-health.

1.

THE COMMON PROBLEMS AND MISHAPS OF CHILDHOOD

When considering the earliest stages of man's development, it is a source of constant amazement to recall how man repeats in his relatively short period of uterine growth the whole evolutionary story of the human race.

Compressed into these first months are the equivalent of millions of years of infinitely slow adaptation, through the different stages of man's growth from the beginning of time.

From the moment of conception, when the primitive fertilized cell rapidly changes from the most simple unicellular creature, the miracle begins and, by processes of division, becomes increasingly more complex as it passes through all the stages of the primitive vertebrate.

At birth it culminates in what must be one of the most significant steps in the history of mankind. The embryo changes from being a totally aquatic creature, developing and confined within a watery environment, to being suddenly able, not just to survive, but to further expand and grow, taking his place permanently as a fully fledged terrestrial or land animal.

Once the break with the tadpole-like existence is complete, man develops and co-ordinates entirely new skills of muscular control, and can rapidly sit up, control his neck and head, crawl, use his limbs, and stand. He becomes a creature of movement, able to travel, contact, and meet other similar terrestrial animals. In early childhood man repeats what is perhaps the supreme achievement of mankind, namely the development of the higher intellectual functions, and the ability to understand, perceive, remember, and to develop language, so that he can communicate verbally with his own kind as he matures. Increasingly, he is able to develop the capacity for intuitive thought, sensitivity and compassion — the supreme hallmark of

Homo Sapiens. With this comes the possibility to express individual and abstract ideas, concepts which contribute to and perhaps eventually help to build a healthy society and culture. This is the miracle of conception, pregnancy and birth.

Just as man in the earliest stages of development passes through an aquatic foetal stage, followed by a terrestrial period of growth, this is reflected in many of the basic remedies used in homoeopathy. Some of the major deeply-acting remedies take their origin from the sea, and have a profound and lasting effect upon the mental and emotional processes which develop during the early weeks of man's existence.

Sepia is one of the most important of the aquatic remedies, acting deeply and over a long period on the reproductive organs, the mind, and the mental processes. Prepared from the ink of the cuttle fish, it is one of the most important of all the female remedies.

Natrum Mur acts strongly upon both the sexes, is prepared from sea-salt or sodium chloride, and is another basic and profound remedy, acting in a broad spectrum way upon the body generally, especially the mental processes and the emotions. This remedy's close link with water and the sea is seen clearly from the swollen, unhealthy looking soft tissues of the face and eyes of the person where the remedy is indicated. The ankles are often swollen and oedematous, and the action of the kidney, the major organ of water control for the body, is weak. *Natrum Mur.* has a tonic and stimulant action upon kidney function and, after the remedy has been taken, there is frequently a powerful elimination of water from the body.

Calcarea comes from the shell of the oyster, and is also a deep and wide-ranging remedy of importance, with a strong action upon the mental and psychological processes. The link with water and the distribution of fluids in the body is clearly seen. The typical patient requiring *Calcarea* is damp-skinned and flabby, as if all the muscles are swimming in an excessive amount of fluid, which undermines their function, tone and strength. Frequently the whole body is streaming with perspiration, and the forehead bathed in sweat.

Iodine is another marine or aquatic remedy, with an effect upon the hormonal functioning, and is related to seaweed.

The important terrestrial or land remedies relate more to the later stages of development, and include many of the mineral and plant remedies such as *Sulphur, Phosphorus, Bryonia* (Wild White Hop), and *Lycopodium* (Club Moss). Such remedies act particularly upon the joints and limbs, the organs of movement and motor function, and generally help to stimulate and cure all the land-related activities — in particular, social interaction, communication, language, eating and swallowing, and any problems of travelling or movement. This may range from a fear of flying, or agoraphobia, to an arthritic problem in a joint or limb. *Rhus Tox.* (Poison Ivy) has a strong effect upon the joints and movement generally, which it eases and stimulates; but it also has an effect upon the tongue and the jaw, the principle organs of verbal communication.

Each child is unique, and there is an enormous variation in patterns of behaviour. Both heredity and environment play major roles, and these differences are experienced and expressed in a variety of diverse ways — levels of vitality and energy; individual likes and dislikes; the shape and proportions of the body; degree of co-ordination; temperament; and the resistance or predisposition to various illnesses. It is this pattern of tendencies which not only makes up the uniqueness of the child, but is also used by the homoeopath to ascertain which remedy best fits or matches the individual pattern of physical and temperamental traits and constitution of the person, and gives the best results in treatment.

The 'constitutional' remedy is always one of the polycrest remedies, or those of a broad sphere of action, stimulating the body's activity over a broad range of physical and mental areas. The physician tends to group the major physical and mental traits of the patient into a broad overall picture, together with aspects of the person which account for his individuality and uniqueness.

The picture includes the physical build, energy levels, mental and physical characteristics, temperament, and any specific likes or dislikes. These together are then matched against the overall symptom patterns of the major polycrest remedies. The particular type of individual pattern of physical traits, vitality and mental aspects, is then named after the polycrest remedy that most resembles it.

This grouping is for convenience of prescribing, and provides a framework to include the predominant individual features of the patient. It is neither rigid nor absolute, particularly in the child who may be a mixture of several remedies, although basically belonging to one group for a majority of his physical traits and attitudes. The constitutional type may change with treatment and maturity. In the adult the make-up is more set and fixed, so that frequently, once the basic constitutional type has been established, it is unvaried. The same basic polycrest remedy will usually help the person and prove effective once its value has been proved in the past. Often, in the adult, the same basic constitutional remedy will prove curative over many years when symptoms arise, and is effective in high potency or dilution, whenever the person is in a low state of vitality. Naturally this varies with the cause and diagnosis of the underlying problem, but often a single dose, given infrequently is enough to keep the person symptom-free and healthy.

Some Constitutional Types in Children

Children who require *Calcarea* are pale, chilly, of flabby build and tending towards obesity. They are often late in all the usual milestones of development, and are frequently nervous, restless and lacking in confidence. They tend to be especially prone to throat infections and diarrhoea. A feature is that they are often unusually fond of eggs, and as infants may show a compulsion to eat certain abnormal substances such as soil, soap, slate, pencils etc.

Phosphorus is indicated in children who are thin, nervous, pale and bright-eyed; usually very popular, social and out-going, yet unduly sensitive, fearful of thunder and new situations, and needing constant reassurance. They love and crave ice-cold food and drinks, and also salt. There is often a chest weakness.

Silicea is of value for the small, pale, thin and chilly child, who is often undersized with sweaty hands and feet, retiring and unsure of himself, though often stubborn in temperament. Usually there is an infection of the throat or ears, with a pusy yellow discharge; and the skin generally is cracked and unhealthy.

Lycopodium helps children who are rather thin and chilly, but who have a dry skin and rarely sweat. They are generally uncompetitive, and more intellectual than sporting. Often they have a worried look about them, associated with problems of indigestion and flatulence from an early age. Usually they crave sweet foods, and have need of company about them because of their dislike and fear of being left alone in the house.

Children where *Natrum Mur.* may be indicated have oily skin and tend to over-salt their food. They are of nervous disposition but do not mind being left alone in the home as they are generally rather independent people. They are often small, undersized and underweight.

Sepia is indicated in sad, often tearful, irritable, rather passive children, always exhausted with no reserves of energy. They tend to be constipated and ravenously hungry with 'dragging down' tummy pains. Such children are always better for a brisk walk or exercise once their initial reluctance has been overcome, and they react well to a social gathering, where they can be the life and soul of the party.

Pulsatilla is indicated in pale, fair-haired, somewhat shy and plump children, usually of passive disposition, but with changeable moods, easily moved to tears at the least thing. There is a marked intolerance of heat and stuffy rooms as they become easily overheated; although, conversely, they can also be very chilly even in summer. Indigestion is common, worse after eating too many starchy pastries, and they are usually restless at night, waking to eat a biscuit or to have a drink. In general they are sensitive, moody, very variable, unpredictable children.

Sulphur helps those children who are warm-blooded, rarely cold and usually rather fat. They may also be thin, but are usually sluggish, red-faced and untidy, with a dislike of water and washing, and are easily irritated. Their favourite food is often fats, in particular butter, which is spread as thickly as possible. On the whole they are difficult, unruly, non-conforming children.

Some children, unfortunately, due to multiple and varied factors, including hereditary influences affecting development during uterine life, or at birth, are damaged in some way. They may be over-active, or mentally subnormal, with a diminished capacity to express, respond and understand. Such cases can be helped provided that the damage is not too severe, and such remedies as *Baryta Carb.* and *Tub. Bov.* are valuable. The latter is especially helpful when there is any history of tuberculous illness in the family, perhaps even several generations back. In general, blockages of mental and physical growth are best dealt with by one of the sea remedies. This is so with Down's Syndrome or mongolism or when there has been an illness in the early weeks of pregnancy, such as German measles or influenza.

Often a remedy such as *Natrum Mur.*, given over a long period in varying strengths, can promote growth and improvement in the general condition. When there has been shock at birth, as with a rapid and precipitate delivery, or perhaps a prolonged delivery with the use of forceps, then the general remedies for shock and head injury are indicated, preferably in high strength. Such remedies include *Arnica, Helleborus* and *Veratrum Alb.* In the last few months of pregnancy, if there is a previous history of miscarriage or threatened abortion, or the uterine functioning is unpredictable, perhaps because of pain or bleeding during the early months, then homoeopathy can help stabilize the uterus and the pregnancy by strengthening and building up normal uterine tone prior to the delivery. In particular, remedies such as *Caulophyllum* are of value in promoting an easier and smoother late pregnancy and delivery.

Childhood is a period of incredibly rapid growth and change. The almost helpless baby infant is born with a powerful instinct to suck and is totally dependent upon the mother for warmth, sustenance and survival. By a rapid process of mental and physical growth the young and increasingly independent child emerges, from an initially compact bundle of primitive reflexes and physiological needs, as the infant, increasingly gaining control over muscular power and co-ordination, and able to express his feelings, needs and emerging personality. Within a few months he has usually learnt to influence his environment, changing from an almost totally passive recipient, to a person, able to express his own demands with increasing force, fullness of character and individuality. These early growth stages are usually subtle and uneventful, merging from one phase to another imperceptibly as the weeks pass.

Some Childhood Problems

FEEDING: Often the young infant has a tendency to suck too fast, and is susceptible to wind, colic and vomiting, not realizing that such urgent and compulsive sucking is not the most efficient way to satisfy his needs. Naturally, hunger quickly follows with a tendency to suck even faster. This excessively powerful sucking reflex, and the recurrent symptoms that tend to arise, are best dealt with in a straightforward way by properly winding the child, slowing the rate of intake, and by giving a few granules of *Nux Vomica*, or *Chamomilla*. The latter is strongly indicated when the child seems bad tempered or irritable.

Sometimes sucking is weak and the child fails to thrive, and does not take either the breast or the bottle strongly. In these cases *China 6* or *Arnica 6* is frequently helpful. Some bottle fed children are allergic to cow's milk and, at an early stage, vomit their food in a projectile fashion, as if shot out of a cannon. In these cases, a few granules of *Aethusa 30* usually relieve the symptoms, and by changing to one of the proprietary milk powders, there is usually no further trouble.

NAPPY RASH: This is best treated by keeping the affected parts dry and clean, with frequent changes of nappy, avoiding enzyme detergents in the wash, and always rinsing the nappies several times after washing. Apply a local soothing cream such as *Calendula* or *Hypercal*, and a few granules of either *Sulphur*, *Rhus Tox.* or *Merc. Sol.* is indicated when the area is more obviously infected rather than just a simple redness and irritation.

TEETHING: This is another very common problem associated with crying, sore gums, irritability and restlessness. Usually the symptoms respond dramatically and quickly to *Chamomilla* when there is marked angry crying, worse for being put down. *Coffea* is another useful remedy when there is severe pain and restless insomnia, while *Aconite* and *Belladonna* may also be required, depending upon the pattern of symptoms.

MINOR ACCIDENTS: As the child grows and explores, falls, grazes, splinters and crushed fingers are all part of the sometimes painful fabric of busy uninhibited childhood. This is where homoeopathy is of enormously rapid and practical benefit in the day-to-day emergencies of the home where there is an active healthy child. An important part of parenthood is to calm, anticipate and protect the busy child, without being over-protective or over-controlling. First-aid problems occur in all families and their treatment is basically straightforward, with a quick response to treatment. A deeply cut wound may need suturing in the casualty department of the local hospital; and any foreign body such as glass, metal, splinters or dirt must be removed before treatment can be effective.

BURNS AND SCALDS: These are best treated by prevention, and anticipating the child, knowing his temperament and taking appropriate action to prevent accidents, particularly when the child is known to be accident-prone. A fireguard is essential, and for an over-active child a railed play area may be necessary at times. This need not be continual, nor develop into a psychological trauma if handled with care and sensitivity. Both *Causticum* and *Cantharis* are important and helpful remedies in the treatment of burns, but if at all severe, the child must be immediately hospitalized.

COUGHS AND COLDS: Such infections are common in childhood and may be complicated by a sore throat or catarrh. When severe and recurrent the conditions usually respond well to *Drosera*, especially when there is associated nausea and sickness. When acute, either *Nux Vomica*, or *Arsenicum* are often curative of the worst symptoms of the common cold, while *Bryonia* is helpful for a dry irritating cough.

EAR INFECTION: Painful, acute middle ear infections are frequent in childhood, and may be associated with enlarged tonsils and recurrent sore throats. The tonsils should not be removed unless absolutely necessary and very severely infected, having failed to respond to a course of homoeopathic treatment. It is usually undesirable and short-sighted to remove one of nature's most important barriers to infection, unless unavoidable. In most cases of acute and very painful middle ear infection, there is a rapid response to *Pulsatilla 30* or *Belladonna 30*. *Aconite* or *Chamomilla* may be needed as an addition in certain cases, depending upon the symptoms and the general picture and condition.

HEADACHES: In young children these are often the sign of anxiety, strain or pressure; of poor light in working conditions, or of fatigue and cold. Sometimes they are the first sign of an acute infective illness such as measles or flu. In general they are best taken lightly, without too much fuss or show of anxiety, but if severe, recurrent and incapacitating, they require thorough investigation and treatment as to their cause, particularly if becoming more frequent.

DIGESTION: Many children suffer from digestive upsets, either from over eating, an infective source, or perhaps a sensitivity to such things as over-ripe fruit or ice-cream. Remedies such as *Phosphorus*, *Arsenicum*, *Podophyllum*, and *Nux Vomica*, should be considered, and these should be a part of the holiday emergency remedies. Some children are compulsive eaters, leading to various digestive problems, and in these cases such remedies as *Calcarea*, *Lycopodium*, and *Pulsatilla* are often indicated, while an allergy to onions may indicate *Thuja* as the remedy of choice.

DIARRHOEA: This is not usually a severe or lasting problem, except in the young baby when dehydration or an excessive loss of fluids may occur. If severe or prolonged, urgent hospitalization may be necessary. Remedies like *Phosphoric Acid*, *Podophyllum*, *Arsenicum* or *China* are often curative, depending upon the type and severity. Blood on the stools may indicate colitis, in which case this is best treated by the doctor, rather than the parents, because of the risk of complications and exacerbations.

CONSTIPATION: This is not very common in childhood except in a febrile condition, when the child has a high temperature or when there is dehydration due to exhausting, prolonged diarrhoea or vomiting. It usually responds well to *Bryonia* or *Nux Vomica*, with a carefully planned diet containing adequate roughage to help redevelop the bowel movement. *Alumina* may be required when there is a sensitivity to aluminium, usually in the kitchen utensils. Often here, the constipation is associated with an eczema and itchy eyes. Changing to stainless steel or enamel cooking utensils is usually effective in curing the constipation.

OBESITY: This is best avoided by paying attention to the diet, and by regular exercise. In some children there may be an underlying hormonal imbalance, when remedies such as *Natrum Mur.*, *Thyroidinum*, *Calcarea*, and *Pulsatilla* are helpful when combined with a calorie controlled diet, and paying attention to any underlying emotional factor. An emotionally insecure child will often eat to gain reassurance, and for comfort when under pressure, either from home or school. In fact, the whole family may be obese and eating too much of the wrong type of diet. If the overweight child is withdrawn, excessively shy and lacking in confidence, expert psychological help may be required to correct the underlying fears.

The basic diet should be as natural and unprocessed as possible (rather than being of foods out of a tin for convenience), and preferably of lightly cooked foods. Foods which nourish and provide energy and natural vitamins without warping the sense of taste should be encouraged, while those that are stodgy, over-seasoned and over-cooked are best avoided. Over-feeding a child with a tendency towards obesity must be avoided at all costs, and usually he will tell the parents when he has had enough. Generally it is good sense to let the child judge how much he should eat, and to stimulate his appetite with varied, attractively prepared, nutritional dishes. We are all susceptible to suggested values as to what we should eat and how much, but having stimulated the taste buds and the imagination of the healthy child, and allowed him to discriminate by providing a sufficiently mixed and broad range of foods, usually, for the active child, 'little and often', is a good working rule.

BEHAVIOURAL PROBLEMS: Should these occur, the situation is best discussed with the child, and if necessary, the school and the teacher concerned. Often a remedy such as *Arg. Nit.* helps and relieves a nervous problem, such as nervous headache or 'Monday morning' tummy ache, especially when there is an associated feeling of fear or terror. Other helpful remedies are *Lycopodium* when the fear is marked, perhaps before a change of school, or a test or examination, while *Silicea* or *Natrum Mur.* may be required for the dramatizing type of child. A change of school may be necessary, or a period of rest away from school in a few severe cases, but usually this is best discussed and agreed with the school, if possible, while giving a remedy according to the individual make-up. A period of psychiatric help may be required with regular treatment, when the problem cannot be resolved with reassurance and discussion, or when the problem has been neglected for a long period.

With a nervous and sensitive child, perhaps under pressure, anxiety may be expressed by the development of certain physical disorders. The type of problem commonly seen is asthma, eczema, perhaps a recurrence of bed-wetting, or sometimes a vague recurrent fever. In others there may be a behaviour disorder or temper-tantrums. Usually there is an obvious cause, and the child is feeling insecure and neglected, perhaps during a pregnancy or after a new baby. The homoeopathic psychological remedies discussed above are usually helpful, and the problem is often easily resolved by the parents provided the child is given adequate attention, and is encouraged to put his fears into words and to bring out into the open whatever is causing the emotional threat. In the case of a pregnancy or a new baby, he should be allowed to share, have a role, and to feel more involved in the new baby.

As they grow and develop, children need plenty of strong, well-made, non-toxic toys, to stimulate interest, absorb attention, develop skills and facilitate new learning and imagination.

During the initial weeks of crawling and walking, some children are unable to manage stairs, and until a good sense of balance and co-ordination has developed, a safety rail may be necessary. Generally it is not recommended to restrict or restrain the growing child, but in the interests of safety this may be necessary in the early months when the child seems to be accident prone. Dangerous drugs, chemicals and toys should be locked away, especially when there is an over-active or seemingly insensitive child. Many children are perfectly sensible and quite safe left in the house or kitchen, while others seem to fall into danger whatever they do and wherever they are. *Kali. Carb.* is helpful for the child who seems naturally clumsy and awkward, always in trouble and minor accidents. When the underlying cause is a need for attention or to be noticed, then *Lycopodium* is indicated. The child requiring *Calcarea* is often slow, awkward, generally off-balance and unprepared, and just not able to react quickly enough. In general the best treatment is prevention by anticipation and avoidance, and to use the indicated remedy when necessary to build up the child. At the same time, sport, games and physical activities can be encouraged to stimulate the sense of judgement, balance, perception and awareness of the position of the body in space and in relation to others. Practise and encouragement can do a great deal to help this type of problem, which can, if neglected, be a handicap for the child at school and with other children.

During this period of rapid growth, with the emergence of physical needs and personality, contact with other children and adults is psychologically essential. The importance of physical contact between parents and child cannot be over-emphasized. Hugging, touching and cuddling are important throughout life, and essential for the young child's normal psychological growth. The presence or lack of it may be a feature in homoeopathic diagnosis and prescribing. The child requiring *Phosphorus* as its basic constitutional remedy has strong needs to be touched, held and stroked, while *Sepia* is indicated for the child averse to being held or temperamentally unable to express himself in any physical way.

Sepia may be equally helpful for the young mother who is unable to develop strong maternal feelings of affection for her new baby and is depressed by her apparent lack of normal maternal feelings. The very young infant cannot verbalize his feelings, and requires contact and physical holding in order to feel together as a person, and to build the foundations for being able to be intimate and affectionate as an adult in later years. The child who has been physically damaged at birth, or who has certain abnormal mental deficiencies, or who has been severely deprived, may be abnormally clinging and physically affectionate, often to a stranger, and in inappropriate and excessive ways. This misplaced and excessive affection is a sign of an underlying inability to discriminate as well as displaying the need for affection and physical closeness.

REST AND SLEEP: These are necessary for us all, and a young child needs a maximum of sleep, and ideally a quiet period just before bedtime, rather than the psychological and physical stimulus of a television programme, particularly if late in the evening. It is important that the parents have time together in the evening on their own without the constant demanding presence of a child; just as the developing child needs to learn to be separate from the parents for some part of the day, either at play school or with other children of his own age. When there is a sleep problem both *Coffea* and *Lycopodium* are frequently helpful.

EXERCISE: Physical activity usually requires no encouragement and is an important way for a child to learn about himself and his family and, from these, about the world in general. He will be seeking to ascertain how far he can extend himself and what are the boundaries of parental tolerance, and at the same time learning how adults respond to his increasing needs, and finding patterns with which to identify or upon which to model his behaviour. Exceptionally, certain children may be excessively over-active. Where this seems severe, to the point where it cannot easily be contained within the bounds of the family, specialized help should be sought to investigate the possible causes and methods of treatment.

All of us need our own space or room, and this is equally true for the child, who should have his own space or playroom as soon as the stage of totally dependent infancy has passed. Loving is not being over-protective, and the child will soon learn to express his basic tastes and personality in his own natural and individual way.

Listening and responding helps to build up experience for the growing child, and is his special way of finding out about the world around him, seeing how others understand and respond to his approaches, messages and signals. By seeing the child as a young person, inexperienced in most areas, but with an enormous potential for learning and development, and in no way an inferior being, helps the adult to put into perspective the apparently unending and meaningless questions that are bombarding him. Parents may often begin to listen again themselves to some of the small child's perceptions, and even learn from them. To some extent, we are all relatively inexperienced in most fields, and immature, although hopefully this lessens as we grow older.

All children have a basic and general need to be looked at, listened to and to gain attention from and have contact with both parents, and other children. This is quite simply a basic part of normal development and not an indulgence or an excess. It is for this reason that it is so important that the couple give their full attention and response to the infant and child, even if not necessarily agreeing with, or approving of, the way he does it. Being noisy and naughty is just one of the ways that the bright and normal child can catch their attention, and the way he uses to provoke and to be noticed.

Learning is curiosity, and the healthy child does this by asking questions. Often the child will answer its own questions, needing attention, admiration and, above all, to get reassurance, a response and a feed-back. This is the basic nourishment for learning and development and the food for all future growth and maturity.

SOME TYPICAL CASES

A girl of eight was brought to me by her mother because she had no resistance and was constantly off school with recurrent coughs and colds. Her ankles were weak and always giving way and she was very pale, not sleeping well because of frequent disturbed dreams — often screaming in her sleep and sleep walking. Because of the disturbed nights it was very difficult to wake her in the morning. She had been slow in developing as a younger child, particularly her teeth which had been slow to come through.

Her hands were cold, damp and clammy and her forehead was frequently covered with sweat at night. Generally she was a good-tempered girl, but rather nervous and lacking in self-confidence.

She was given a 10M of *Calcarea*, and when seen a month later there had been a marked improvement, with a lessening of the nervousness. She was sleeping better and the pallor was no longer so noticeable.

*   *   *

A three year old boy was seen because of recurrent colds, throat and nose infections every three weeks since the family had moved to England from Australia about two years before. The nasal discharge was yellow or green, and he was frequently coughing during the day, but usually slept well. He was an overactive child, unable to keep still, extremely nervous and apprehensive. He was thin, pale, wiry, did not sweat much and was on the whole rather tidy. Generally he seemed to need a great deal of holding and attention and he rarely took his eyes off me.

The mother described him as being irritable and often stubborn and dis-obedient, rather self-willed and very tidy, rarely crying. He did not feel the cold much, and was not particularly thirsty.

He was given *Phosphorus 10M* and not seen until seven months later when the mother reported that he had improved considerably and was more manageable, but as there had been a mild recurrence of the symptoms she requested a further dosage of *Phosphorus* which had helped him so much.

*   *   *

A child aged eight years was brought to me who had a six-year history of eczema, mainly on the legs and in the flexor creases of the knees, causing a lot of itching, irritation and scratching at night.

A year after the onset of the eczema she had developed asthma, although this had been only mild for the past two years, but she had now developed hay fever over this period when the wheezing was better.

She was a very engaging little girl, with pale blonde hair, fair skin and blue eyes, slightly shy, and usually somewhat of a loner with few friends. At times she was defiant and stubborn, but on the whole she was easy-going and fairly quiet and placid.

Another of her problems was travel sickness, always brought on by travelling in the front of the car.

She could not tolerate hot weather, or sitting in the direct sun, and preferred cool weather generally, never complaining in the winter. Most of her symptoms were worse in the summer. She was a child who cried easily and was very emotional — intolerant of all fats, which worsened her skin condition. She was given *Pulsatilla*, and when seen two months later the mother reported that she was much less irritable, and that the eczema was beginning to improve.

*   *   *

Another case of eczema was that of a boy aged five, with a history of eczema since the age of six months, and asthma developing at the age of eighteen months following pneumonia.

The child was small, wiry, red-faced, untidy, rarely still, and covered with a dry harsh eczematous rash over both arms, elbows and hands, in the groin, lower abdomen, and behind the knees.

The skin was extremely itchy and always worse at night with the heat of the bed. He rarely cried, was very fond of all foods, liking butter and fats, quite a bit of salt and having a sweet tooth for chocolates and cakes. Generally water aggravated the condition.

He was given *Sulphur 10M*. When next seen the mother reported a slight improvement, but reported that there was still a great deal of itching and irritation. *Psorinum 6* was prescribed and some *Hypercal* cream given to apply locally.

On his next visit, the skin was softer and less dry and the legs were almost cleared completely of the rash.

*   *   *

An infant of eighteen months was brought to see me by both parents — because he had been off his food for two weeks, refusing to be fed and rejecting everything the mother offered him. The stools were green, loose and soft. He was teething, screaming most of the time, generally irritable and bad-tempered, and waking in the night screaming.

Usually he was a happy child, but for the last two weeks he had been whining, wanting to be cuddled, and had a slight dry cough.

The child was given *Chamomilla 200* in three doses, with an immediate response — calming down and falling asleep in the surgery. Forty-eight hours later the father rang me to say that he was completely better, sleeping and eating normally, and that there was no recurrence of the screaming fits of rage and irritation.

*   *   *

A first baby of ten weeks was seen with both parents because the right hip joint was suspected of having a congenital abnormality. The joint was 'clicking' and generally too loose and mobile. An X-ray showed no abnormal findings. The child was given *Calcarea 10M* — in a single dosage.

Two months later the mother reported that the hip was improving but the baby was sick after food, and that the vomit was projectile, spouting out with considerable force.

She was given *Aethusa* in a single dose and, when seen in a further two months, the hip symptoms had completely cleared, and she was taking her feeds perfectly normally, gaining weight and no longer vomiting.

*   *   *

A child of two-and-a-half was seen because of a dry, irritating barking and hacking cough, worse at night and not improving over a period of about a month. The coughing came in bouts which were so severe that they almost led to vomiting. *Drosera 6* at night improved the cough markedly, but did not completely clear it.

The mother reported that she was a mouth breather and often had a slightly infected eye in the morning on waking, and that she cried a lot.

She tolerated heat well and had had an ear infection a few months previously. Generally she took a lot of salt with her food, and her eyes were always watering, particularly when out walking on a windy day.

Natrum Mur. was given with an immediate positive response.

*   *   *

Another case was of a child aged five with a history of recurrent middle ear infections following measles the previous summer. Immediately afterwards she complained of deafness — and soon after she had developed several acute painful attacks — always in the right ear. The specialist she had seen privately had diagnosed deafness in both the high and low decibel frequencies on testing.

She was a rather warm, slightly plump child, with damp hands and often damp around the head and forehead at night. She was slightly slower than the other children and rather untidy, fearful shy and quiet, anxious about new things, often quite restless, fiddling with her clothes a lot. She liked eggs and they were her favourite food. She preferred the warm weather and could take the sun.

Calcarea 10M was prescribed, and when next seen she was coughing, waking at 4.30 am, with a hard dry cough. *Kali. Bich. 6* was given with an immediate improvement. Her general condition changed markedly, there were no further attacks of otitis media and when she was seen for a specialist opinion four months later, both the ear drums and the audiogram hearing tests were normal.

*   *   *

A child aged five was seen with a three-year history of 'nervous tummy' attacks, lasting four to six weeks, when she was not interested in eating and sick in her sleep, usually between 10 pm and midnight, after a quiet 'droopy' day associated with tummy ache.

She was always a poor sleeper and could not get off to sleep since her parents divorced three years earlier.

There were no abnormal findings on physical examination. She was a sensitive child, outgoing and friendly, but rather nervous and over-anxious in general. She did not cry much, and needed a lot of cuddling and reassurance. She tended to be thirsty, quite liked salt, fats and cream, not tolerating the heat very well — generally feeling better for being at the seaside. She was given *Natrum Mar. 10M* and remained well and symptom-free for almost a year, when the remedy was again repeated in the same potency, and there has been no recurrence of the symptoms for a further fifteen months, when she was last seen.

*   *   *

There was a child who I saw at the age of eight with a history of eczema, which started at only two days old, on the cheeks and chest, followed by asthma at two-and-a-half years, and bed-wetting at night, since the age of five, treated without response by the pad and buzzer method. The onset was during the mother's pregnancy with a younger brother.

He was a lively, bright, affectionate boy, popular and good at sports, rather thirsty and liking cold drinks. He generally preferred cool weather to the heat.

When first seen there was a mild eczematous, itchy rash behind the knees and at times behind the ears, the chest was moderately wheezy. He was allergic to eggs and chocolate.

The skin generally was very dry and he had a marked tendency to sweat around the head at night.

He was given *Phosphorus 10M* and three weeks later the mother reported a marked improvement in the chest and in his catarrhal symptoms.

This was followed by *Calc. Sulph.* when there was an immediate lessening of the rash, with absence of itching and generally he was more cheerful.

He remained well for several months until some wheeziness returned in the heat of the summer. *Phosphorus* was repeated again and this time was followed by a much longer period without asthma.

The bed-wetting improved more slowly, and lessened as treatment progressed.

TREATMENT INDEX

Asthma

Definition   Usually an acute spasmodic condition, characterized by paroxysms of wheezy, difficult breathing and tightness in the chest. May become chronic.

Causes   Usually unknown, often said to be of allergic, emotional or familial origin. No consistent causes, but better from change of environment.

Symptoms   Tightness of the chest, anxiety, fatigue, laboured audible expiratory phase, with high pitched wheeze. Perspiration, and grey, yellow, or white cast-like sputum.

Treatment   *Phosphorus; Kali. Carb.; Medorrhinum; Arsenicum; Cuprum Arsen.; Cuprum Aceticum; Nux Vomica; Sulphur; Aconite; Ipecacuanha.*

Phosphorus   One of the best and most reliable remedies, with noisy wheezy breathing, oppression, cough, in a tall thin narrow chested person. They are nearly always anxious, and need a lot of reassurance and attention.

Kali. Carb.   There is severe wheezing, and shortness of breath, worse at night in the early evening and in the morning, worse for dust, central heating, and usually associated with anxiety and weakness.

Medorrhinum   There is a dry cough, and shortness of breath, worse for lying down, and better for kneeling face down, or lying on the stomach. Useful in chronic difficult recurrent cases. Not to be repeated for a period of six months after the initial prescription.

Arsenicum   Short anxious breathing, worse on lying down, pale face, burning heat in the chest, cold sweats, prostration.

Cuprum Arsen.   There is severe shortness of breath, a sense of constriction and weight about the chest, and often pain under the left shoulder blade. The patient is usually icy-cold, and covered with sweat.

Cuprum Aceticum There is the most distressing dry cough, together with shortness, weakness, and restlessness. All symptoms are worse just after midnight and for sitting upright.

Nux Vomica Spasm of the bronchi, irritability, tongue has yellow coating, nausea, flatulence, constipation.

Sulphur For chronic cases, with a recurrent cough, the expectoration of a foul thick mucous, and often failure to respond to earlier well-indicated remedies.

Aconite In plethoric individual, with anxiety, dyspnoea, after exposure to wind and cold, or chill.

Ipecacuanha Tightness in the chest, and loud rattling cough, sweating cold and restless, anxious, nausea.

Bed-Wetting (Nocturnal Enuresis)

Definition The inability to control the bladder function in sleep, so that there is the involuntary passing of urine in the night.

Causes Almost without exception, the cause is psychological in nature.

Symptoms In general, the only physical symptom is of the involuntary passage of urine during sleep. In addition the child is usually sensitive, and there are added problems of shame and guilt.

Treatment *Sabadilla; Lycopodium; Ferr. Phos.; Arsenicum; Gelsemium; Belladonna.*

Sabadilla A useful remedy to consider for general problems of bladder weakness. The urine is often thick and clay-coloured.

Lycopodium The urine is loaded with uric acid.

Ferr. Phos. The urine has a coffee smell to it, and there is often involuntary loss on coughing. When there is weakness of the sphincter muscles it is indicated.

Arsenicum A useful remedy when prescribed constitutionally in high potency for the over-conscientous child, neat, with obsessional personality features and always thin, chilly, and excessively anxious.

Gelsemium Useful in nervous, hysterical children.

Belladonna When the bed-wetting occurs in the early night hours.

Chicken Pox

Definition   A usually mild infectious disease, of viral origin.

Causes   Infection by the Varicella virus, caused by contact with either a carrier or an acute case.

Symptoms   Characteristic vesicles, filled with watery fluid on the second day, drying up on the third and fourth day, to form scabs or crusts. Fever is mild and short lasting, no scars.

Treatment   *Aconite; Rhus Tox.; Ant. Tart.; Belladonna; Apis; Sulphur; Mercurius; Gelsemium; Pulsatilla.*

Aconite   In the febrile stage, with symptoms of anxiety, fear, thirst, dry heat, rapid, hard and full pulse.

Rhus Tox.   The first remedy to be prescribed, in the early stages. Restless in mind and body. It arrests the progress of the disease.

Ant. Tart.   Helps the development of the vesicle, and of value when the eruption is slow to form, and also when there is cough and cold.

Belladonna   Headache, flushing, sore throat, fever, circum-oral pallor.

Apis   Excessive itching of the eruption.

Sulphur   Hungry, eats little. Very thirsty.

Mercurius   For any infection of the chicken pox vesicles.

Gelsemium   When the fever is slow to fall, the patient is weak, drowsy and dizzy.

Pulsatilla   Mild, tearful, thirstless form of the illness.

Colic (Intestinal)

Definition   Severe constriction and spasm of the circular smooth muscle of the intestinal wall.

Causes   Usually due to dietary indiscretion, or food poisoning, or emotional factors in some temperaments.

Symptoms   Mainly sudden griping, intermittent pain, in the umbilical area, doubling-up, better for deep pressure and heat.

Treatment   *Chamomilla; Nux Vomica; Colocynth; Belladonna; Plumbum Met.; Bryonia; Ipecacuanha; Mag. Carb.; Veratum Album; Mag. Phos.*

Chamomilla   Twisting, pinching pain, 'tearing' around navel, diarrhoea, better with local heat and at night, irritability.

Nux Vomica   Severe cramps, flatulence, constipation, spasmodic pains from over-eating, better sitting or lying down.

Colocynth   Griping intermittent pains, with flatulence, tenesmus and diarrhoea, cannot keep still, colic in the navel area, better for firm pressure, flatulence, anxious.

Belladonna   Better for leaning forward.

Plumbum Met.   Violent colic, umbilical, with flatus, better for doubling-up, obstinate constipation, shooting pains, face pale, extremities cold.

Bryonia   Colic severe, bowels distended, stitching pains, worse for movement, jar, touch, heat, diarrhoea, lies motionless, knees drawn up.

Ipecacuanha   Colic in the pit of the stomach, associated with nausea, restlessness and often worse for the least movement.

Mag. Carb.   There is a generalized colic over the whole abdominal area, with diarrhoea, and often very considerable abdominal distension and tightness.

Veratum Alb.   The pain is severe, relieved by a bowel movement, the whole abdomen is tender and often distended, the skin cold and sweating.

Mag. Phos.   The colic is severe, radiating upwards, and better for heat locally applied. A watery diarrhoea is commonly present.

Coughs

Definition   Spasmodic contractions of the diaphragm, due to irritation of the respiratory tract, from a variety of causes.

Causes   Irritation of the soft palate and upper respiratory tract, particularly from infection or foreign body.

Symptoms   Cough is a symptom itself, and not a disease, the type of cough is very variable in type and characteristics, affecting choice of remedy.

Treatment   *Aconite; Belladonna; Bryonia; Ipecacuanha; Drosera; Spongia Tosta; Hepar Sulph.; Phosphorus; Chamomilla; Sulphur; Kali. Bich.*

Aconite   Dry hard cough, constant, acute, worse at night, better for cold, anxious, restless, face flushed, constipation, worse from exposure to cold winds.

Belladonna   Short dry shaking cough, violent paroxysms of coughing, larynx dry, worse at night. Flushed face, headache.

Bryonia   Hard, dry, shaking cough, worse in daytime, often with pain in the side and stitches in chest, holds head and chest when coughing, desires large quantities of cold water.

Ipecacuanha   A moist rattling cough, worse at night, often associated with vomiting and anxiety. The chest sounds wheezy.

Drosera   Violent throat tickle and cough. Spasmodic cough, worse at night, with retching, gagging and vomiting, may be blood-streaked sputum, perspires on waking, pain below ribs.

Spongia Tosta   Dry barking, whistling cough, with tickling, hoarseness, loss of voice, better after eating and drinking.

Hepar Sulph.   Cough due to infection, often bronchitis, with wheezing, lack of air, and weakness. There is often a high temperature, the child toxic.

Phosphorus   The typical cough is dry and irritating, worse at night, preventing sleep, and often associated with a history or tendency to asthma.

Chamomilla   There is a dry irritating cough, worse at night, with restlessness, irritability and sometimes wheezing. Often provoked by a fit of anger.

Sulphur   The cough is moist and rattling, productive of a dirty-looking, thick, greenish-yellow infected sputum. Useful for chronic conditions.

Kali. Bich.   Cough with tough stringy expectoration, wheezing, dizziness, worse after meals, on getting up in the morning, may be blood-streaked.

Diarrhoea

Definition   The frequent passage of liquid motions, the stools unformed and often offensive, sometimes containing slime and blood.

Causes   Over-eating, infection, chill, excitement.

Symptoms   Repeated loose, very soft, or liquid stools, varying in colour, odour. Often associated with loss of appetite, colic, nausea, sweating, coated tongue, weakness.

Treatment   *Pulsatilla; Arsenicum; Ipecacuanha; China; Phosphoric Acid; Podophyllum.*

Pulsatilla   Stools changeable and variable, worse evening, follows fatty/starchy food. Weepy.

Arsenicum   Severe diarrhoea, burning, watery, with much mucus, and often green or pale in colour. There is nearly always associated vomiting, collapse, and chill.

Ipecacuanha   The stools are usually fermented, green or yellow, and have an offensive smell. Often worse in the autumn. Colic is common.

China   There is a pale, mucous and slimy diarrhoea, often worse after eating fruit, worse at night. An involuntary discharge of faeces may occur.

Phosphoric Acid   Painless, chronic diarrhoea, slimy yellow pale stools, often with involuntary loss, particularly when moving about. This is an excellent remedy for acute painless diarrhoea.

Podophyllum   One of the major remedies for severe chronic diarrhoea, particularly worse in the early morning. The stool is watery, unformed, contains mucus, green, and associated with weakness and colic.

Ear Ache

Definition	In children this is usually an infection of the middle ear.
Causes	Usually follows a chill or exposure to draught, but often cause is unknown.
Symptoms	Severe, unbearable, throbbing pain, fever, sweating, redness, headache.
Treatment	*Aconite; Belladonna; Pulsatilla; Mercurius; Chamomilla; Sulphur; Merc. Sol.; Hepar Sulph.; Plantago.*
Aconite	Acute onset, pain, fever, better local heat.
Belladonna	Headache, sore throat, throbbing ear ache, right sided, redness of face. Worse least jar, better heat, no thirst.
Pulsatilla	Darting, tearing, variable pains, catarrh following measles. Caused by chill when warm and getting wet. Weepy craves company.
Mercurius	The pains are severe, sharp and lancing, often with an icy sensation in the ear, and a discharge of pus or blood. The temperature is often high, and the child toxic, sweating profusely, and restless.
Chamomilla	Irritable, cross and fretful, very severe unbearable pains, pricking. Worse local heat, better if carried.
Sulphur	Useful for recurrent ear aches with an offensive discharge and burning sensations, and stitch-like pains which come and go.
Merc. Sol.	Pains extend to the teeth, worse from warm bed, throbbing pains, enlarged glands.
Hepar Sulph.	Stitching pains, sore throat, chilly, peevish and irritable. Worse from the least draught, often starts left ear and then moves to right ear.

Plantago Tincture Use locally, if there is no discharge from the ear.

Eczema

Definition A catarrhal inflammation of the skin, characterized by redness, irritation, multiple small vesicles, serous discharge, and crusting.

Causes Unknown, but often hereditary. Associated with asthma, hay-fever and other allergic phenomena. Stress is a precipitating factor.

Symptoms Pain, itching, smarting, discomfort.

Treatment *Sulphur; Rhus Tox.; Psorinum; Graphites; Mezereum.*

Sulphur One of the best remedies, with scratching, itching a rough red irritable skin, often infected. The eczema is always worse for water, and often the irritation is aggravated at night by the heat of the bed. An early morning offensive diarrhoea is also characteristic.

Rhus Tox. For a dry red itchy eczema on the hand and wrists, often with multiple vesicle formation. Irritation and tingling is considerable, and usually the eruption is worse at night or in damp weather, better for heat.

Psorinum The skin is very irritable, and has a grey, greasy unwashed dirty appearance. Irritation in the folds of the knee and elbow, often with infection of the skin in the eczematous area.

Graphites The eruption is present on the scalp and particularly behind the ears, oozing a honey-like discharge. The scalp and area affected itches considerably.

Mezereum Often affects the scalp with infected crusty vesicles which may ooze and itch severely.

Food Poisoning

Definition	Acute infection of the intestinal tract by the salmonella organism.
Causes	Infected food, failure to adequately cook infected frozen food, and re-heating it, lack of general hygiene in the kitchen, not covering and refrigerating in the summer.
Symptoms	Severe diarrhoea and vomiting, collapse, weakness, sweating.
Treatment	*Arsenicum; Bryonia; Pulsatilla; Carbo Veg.; China; Nux Vomica; Colocynth; Mag. Phos.; Podophyllum; Phosphoric Acid.*
Arsenicum	Cold, chilly, great weakness and prostration, sometimes blood in the stool.
Bryonia	Nausea and vomiting, with colic and diarrhoea. The patient lies immobile, pale and the least pressure or movement worsens the pains.
Pulsatilla	Thirstless, due to excessive starchy foods, conditions and symptoms very variable.
Carbo Veg.	Nausea and vomiting with a constipated stool, cramping upper abdominal pains, worse at night and after eating. Flatulence and distension is a marked feature. Collapse.
China	Weakness is always a marked feature, with colic, vomiting and painless diarrhoea, often at night. Worse or provoked by eating fruit (unripe usually is the cause).
Nux Vomica	When due to indigestible foods and irritable.
Colocynth	Enteritis with colic, worse in the morning.
Mag. Phos.	Also for colic.
Podophyllum	For severe watery diarrhoea.
Phosphoric Acid	For epidemic Summer diarrhoea.

Foreign Body in the Ear

Definition   The presence of any foreign object in the outer ear passage e.g. pea, bead, insect.

Causes   Non-specific, and part of childish curiosity about the body.

Symptoms   Pain, irritation, deafness, wax.

Treatment   Remove with cotton wool bud or gentle means with *Arnica* lotion.

Arnica Lotion   The local application reduces the swelling and inflammatory response of the local tissues to the irritation, and facilitates the removal of the offending body, by opening-up the orifice. When there is severe bruising and inflammation, *Arnica* should also be taken internally in the sixth potency for a few days.

Foreign Body in the Eye

Definition	The presence of any foreign substance on the eye, and usually under the eyelid. e.g. fly, sand.
Causes	Non-specific and common, failure to take precautions.
Symptoms	Pain, irritation, conjunctivitis, watering of the eye.
Treatment	*Arnica* lotion; *Arnica*.
Arnica Lotion	A weak solution externally after removal of foreign body.
Arnica	The internal administration of *Arnica* for a few days helps to reduce any swelling or bruising of delicate tissues, and reduces any inflammatory reactions to a minimum, without preventing the normal healing reaction of the body to the irritation. It also helps to prevent any infection in this delicate area.

Growing Pains

Definition   Pains in the limbs of the young child or adolescent, not associated with any underlying disease process.

Causes   Aching in the legs and arms, often at night, intermittent, no fever associated. Cause unknown.

Treatment   *Calcarea; Calc. Phos.; Phosphoric Acid.*

Calcarea   This is indicated for the rather pale, overweight child, somewhat phlegmatic, when drawing or stinging pains occur in the knees or ankles, often after walking. Cramp is common after any prolonged period of sitting. Usually the child was late in learning to walk.

Calc. Phos.   This is indicated for a much thinner child, easily exhausted, with odd pains in the hips, shins, and in the joints in general. Walking is often late.

Phosphoric Acid   There is a bruised sensation, stitch-like, and worse for walking or on waking. Weakness of the legs is commonly associated.

Hernia (Congenital)

Definition   A small pouching of the abdominal layers and intestine through the skin wall.

Causes   Congenital weakness in the paraumbilical area.

Symptoms   Small localized swelling, which can be reduced back into the abdominal cavity.

Treatment   *Calc. Carb.; Nux Vomica;* Local pressure pad and bandage.

Calc. Carb.   When there is an associated hydrocele.

Nux Vomica   Helpful in hernia generally.

Infected Wounds

Definition	Inflammatory changes in a wound, with infection.
Causes	Local infection, usually associated with the trauma.
Symptoms	Heat, swelling, pain, redness, fever.
Treatment	*Staphysagria; Hypericum* tincture locally; *Aconite; Belladonna; Silicea; Hepar Sulph.*
Staphysagria	The wound is usually very painful, with an itching tearing, drawing, almost unbearable in character. Anger and resentment is always a feature.
Hypericum tincture	This may be applied locally in early cases.
Aconite	Is indicated in early acute cases of infection with redness, fever and swelling.
Belladonna	This may follow *Aconite* when there is great heat, redness, fever, and swelling and tenderness.
Silicea	When there is chronic infection and pus formation, not responding to treatment.
Hepar Sulph.	When there is pus formation and infection.

Impetigo

Definition A severe contagious condition of children and adults, with a severe purulent inflammation and pustules of the skin.

Causes Infection, poor environment, overcrowding, poor diet, constitutional.

Symptoms The pustular eruption is on the face, head, scalp, often with a crusty discharge.

Treatment *Sulphur; Mezereum; Arsenicum; Silicea; Ant. Crud.*

Sulphur One of the most useful remedies initially.

Mezereum When there is much oozing and scab formation on the scalp.

Arsenicum Useful generally, particularly when debility is marked.

Silicea Helpful when there is infection and cold damp extremities in a thin chilly child.

Ant. Crud. Useful when there is chronic infection not responding to treatment.

Insect Stings

Definition The skin is penetrated by the sting of the insect, usually a wasp, bee, hornet or ant. In some areas the horse-fly can also cause very painful and inflammatory reactions.

Causes There is an inflammatory response to the chemical toxin in the sting, which is a severe irritant to the area surrounding the point of entry of the sting.

Symptoms Pain, swelling, redness. There may be a more generalized allergic response in some sensitive people, with collapse, breathlessness, palpitations, and very severe painful constricting local oedema.

Treatment *Apis; Ledum; Calendula* tincture, or *Ledum* tincture locally; *Arnica*, or *Hypercal*. The initial treatment is always to remove the sting or barb as soon as possible, often by scraping the skin surface. Always treat the shock if there is any evidence of collapse or severe allergic response.

Apis When due to a bee-sting or mosquito, with local swelling, redness, irritation, and pain. Little urine is passed during the period of the acute pain, and this is a quite specific indication for *Apis*.

Ledum This is indicated for a fairly localized penetrating sting, where there is pain and irritation, without the redness and swelling of *Apis*.

Arnica This is essential when there is any degree of shock, or collapse, or when the area feels bruised, and sore, and where the swelling is less red and itching than with *Apis*.

Calendula tincture Apply when there is any possibility of infection developing, as with a sting in a soiled area of the body, as might occur when working in the garden.

Ledum tincture Apply locally when there is a deep and painful penetrating sting.

Hypercal cream Apply to the area, in order to encourage healing and to reduce the pain and irritation in the area.

Itching

Definition	Itching of the skin, often distressing, and associated with eczema.
Causes	Allergic, eczema, unknown, familial, worms, head lice.
Symptoms	Intolerable itching, and scratching, and redness, bleeding.
Treatment	*Pulsatilla; Arsenicum; Sulphur; Merc. Sol.; Psorinum.*
Pulsatilla	Itching worse at night for the heat of the bed. Usually thirstless, the symptoms vary a lot and are periodic.
Arsenicum	Useful in the chilly child, with eczema and burning itching. Thirst is a characteristic.
Sulphur	This remedy is also a basic one, and has burning and itching, redness, usually eczema associated and worse for water.
Merc. Sol.	Particularly useful in a chronically infected skin condition, with recurrent eruptions, which ooze, and are chronically sore and irritating.
Psorinum	The skin looks greasy and somewhat dirty. This is one of the best remedies for itching in the flexure creases of the elbows and knees.

Lice

Definition	Infection of the scalp with the parasite Pediculus capitis.
Causes	Contagion, lack of hygiene, overcrowding.
Symptoms	Itching and irritation of the scalp and the presence of parasites in the hair.
Treatment	*Sabadilla* shampoo (prepared from tincture) daily, one part in twenty; *Natrum Mur.; Staphysagria; Tub. Bov.*
General	Strict hygiene is essential.
Sabadilla tincture	In daily shampoo is very helpful.
Natrum Mur.	Indicated when the condition is present on a greasy scalp, often with dandruff, and a marked irritating eruption around the hair-line usually on the forehead area.
Staphysagria	The scalp is severely itching and constantly irritating, and is always being touched or scratched and infected and re-infected. There is also frequently, an infection, which gives a dirty-looking oozing, moist discharge, and the least examination of the area causes anger, opposition and rage.
Tub. Bov.	This is often curative in chronic cases.

Measles

Definition   An acute infectious disease of children.

Causes   Direct contact, incubation period of 10-14 days.

Symptoms   Always catarrhal onset, cold, infected eyes, headache,
                    hoarseness, cough, fever, followed after five days by a
                    blotchy rash, first on face, then neck and chest.

Treatment   *Morbillimum; Pulsatilla; Aconite; Gelsemium; Bryonia;
                    Euphrasia; Ferrum Phos.*

Morbillimum   *Morbillimum 200* is prophylactic, and of value in the on-
                    going treatment.

Pulsatilla   Generally very helpful when the case is thirstless,
                    restless and irritable. Cough worse in the evening, with
                    yellow catarrhal discharge from throat and nose.
                    Diarrhoea, intestinal and gastric upsets.

Aconite   If there is a high fever, full pulse, dry cough,
                    constipation, restlessness and thirst.

Gelsemium   Treats the complications, of high fever, and suppressed
                    eruptions. Often thirsty, constipation, headache,
                    delirium, prostrated, dry tongue. Convulsions may
                    occur.

Bryonia   Dry hacking cough.

Euphrasia   Streaming nose and eyes, photophobia, eyes sore,
                    moderate temperature.

Ferrum Phos.   The skin is warm, hot and burning, usually the throat is
                    painful and swollen. There is intolerance to any form of
                    heat, or warmth, yet the least cold draught or cool air is
                    intolerable. Although the skin is burning, the patient
                    often feels very chilled.

Mumps

Definition   An acute contagious, epidemic infection of parotid and salivary glands. Mainly affects children and young adults.

Causes   Direct contagion by contact, during epidemic, more rarely isolated cases occur, very common in spring and summer.

Symptoms   Swelling, heat, pain, fever at the angle of the jaw, dysphagia. Usually worse on fourth day and better by tenth day.

Treatment   *Aconite; Pulsatilla; Belladonna; Rhus Tox.; Sulphur; Hepar Sulph.; Pilocarpin Mur.; Parotidinum.*

Aconite   When there is fever, restlessness, thirst, pain, in the acute early stages.

Pulsatilla   When the testicles or breasts are involved.

Belladonna   When the parotitis is right-sided, with fever, redness and swelling.

Rhus Tox.   When the parotitis is left-sided, with swelling and erythema, worse from cold and damp. Also for prevention when contact is suspected.

Sulphur   Needed if infection becomes a complication of the illness.

Hepar Sulph.   Only of value for suppuration and severe infective complications.

Pilocarpinum Mur.   As a preventative.

Parotidinum   As a preventative.

Nose-Bleed (Epistaxis)

Definition	The spontaneous nose-bleed, not due to a blow.
Causes	Nose-picking in the child, haemophilia, but usually occurs spontaneously.
Symptoms	Sudden onset of nose-bleeding (usually from one side), weakness, fainting, anaemia and pallor may be associated.
Treatment	*Hamamelis* internally and *Hamamelis* tincture externally; *Aconite; Belladonna; Arnica; Vipera 200; Pulsatilla; Ferrum Phos.; Arsenicum.*
Hamamelis	Externally as tincture, and internally in pill form.
Aconite	In plethoric make-up, due to excitement.
Belladonna	Due to cerebral congestion, preceded by throbbing headache in temples.
Arnica	Indicated for the very severe form when there is shock.
Vipera 200	This remedy specifically for clotting and the arrest of haemorrhage.
Pulsatilla	When associated with sudden amenorrhoea, and takes the place of the monthly flow.
Ferrum Phos.	If profuse bright red blood, clots easily.
Arsenicum	Very agitated, restless, anxious and prostrated.

Otitis Media

Definition   Acute middle ear infection.

Causes   Acute infection, usually from throat, or blood borne.

Symptoms   Fever, acute pain, may be throbbing.

Treatment   (This is an acute condition which should be treated by the physician as soon as possible.)
Belladonna; Aconite; Chamomilla; Mercurius; Pulsatilla.

Belladonna   One of the earliest and most acute remedies when there is a very severe attack with sudden boring pains, tearing pains, fever, sweating. The ear drum is infected and often tense. The symptoms are worse at night and better for warm applications.

Aconite   For very early acute cases with fever, severe stinging pain, often throbbing due to a chill or sudden change of temperature. All symptoms are worse at night and worse for warmth.

Chamomilla   For pricking, unbearably violent, severe pain and irritation. Cheeks are red, and the patient is restless, worse at night and from the cold.

Mercurius   There are severe pains, a high temperature, and often the discharge of pus, the child is restless, crying, often sweating and may be delirious. There is a frequent and quite specific sensation of icy cold water in the ear which is the clearest indication for the remedy.

Pulsatilla   A very useful remedy for ear infection. The ear is painful, hot and inflamed, with pains which come and go and are very variable. There is often a yellow greenish discharge. All symptoms are worse for heat. The patient is very tearful and thirstless, with a temperature.

Scarlatina

Definition	An acute, contagious, infectious disease.
Causes	An acute toxic reaction, involving the skin and the body generally due to a throat infection by the haemolytic streptococcus bacterium.
Symptoms	Sudden onset, high fever, hot flushes, nausea and thirst, irritability. Scarlet rash, begins on the chest, spreading to the whole body. Sore throat, and tongue red and raw.
Treatment	*Belladonna; Sulphur; Arsenicum; Aconite.*
Belladonna	Usually follows *Aconite*, during the red eruption. Also is prophylactic. Three doses to prevent the illness is usually sufficient.
Sulphur	The skin is hot, red and itching, the rash slow to clear, and when *Sulphur* is indicated, some of the areas have become infected, or cracked, or discharging pus. The body is typically hot but in general there is an intolerance to any form of water applied to the skin.
Arsenicum	Used as the fever is declining.
Aconite	Initially during the high fever, and if excitement is a marked feature.

School Phobia

Definition   Fear of leaving home and its security to attend school.

Causes   Always psychological. The child may be over-protected, with an over-anxious mother. Rigid school, lack of confidence, previous illness.

Symptoms   Anxiety, and paralysing fear and terror of dying, collapsing, fainting, palpitations, sweating, abdominal pains, panic.

Treatment   *Argent. Nit.; Gelsemium; Lycopodium.*

Argent. Nit.   One of the best remedies, the patient is fearful, lacks confidence in everything he attempts, and tends to over-idealize others, which increases his fear of them. Typically time passes slowly, and he feels threatened by solitude, although any demands on his attention by others provokes feelings of rage and resentment. Heat in any form is oppressive.

Gelsemium   Useful remedy in phobic conditions, often when there is a hysterical component, with clinging to the parents, irritability, great sense of fatigue and exhaustion, and fear of solitude in any form. Although there is a dislike for heat, it is not so severe as the complete intolerance shown where *Arg. Nit.* is indicated.

Lycopodium   The school phobia is part of a general pattern of fear and of the anticipation of disaster. It is indicated when there is a change of school, or the problem has been precipitated by a new situation. The child is nearly always artistic and sensitive, showing a marked degree of hypochondriasis, often learned from one of the parents.

Skin Troubles (Cracking)

Definition   The condition of skin cracking, often at the finger tips and hands. Sometimes involves the anal region.

Causes   Usually unknown.

Symptoms   Cracking of the finger tips, and hands, often chronic and failing to heal.

Treatment   *Silicea; Petroleum; Natrum Mur.; Agaricus; Sulphur; Tamus* tincture.

Silicea   This is a valuable remedy when there is cracking at the tips of the fingers which are deep and fail to heal. The extremities are usually cold and sweaty.

Petroleum   There is a thick chronic eczema, dirty-looking and often thick with harsh red, dry skin, which tends to crack.

Natrum Mur.   The area around the nails may crack and become infected or develop 'hang-nail' infections.

Agaricus   For winter chilblains which are red, painful and itching with a tendency to crack. The circulation is poor.

Sulphur   Has a dirty-looking red itchy skin, which may crack and is always aggravated by water.

Tamus tincture   A useful remedy for local application.

Sore Throat

Definition	Soreness and swelling of the throat, of infective origin.
Causes	Infection, anaemia, trauma, measles.
Symptoms	Pain, redness, difficulty in swallowing, often associated with fever.
Treatment	*Belladonna; Mercurius; Aconite; Baryta Carb.; Dulcamara; Hepar Sulph.; Merc. Sol.; Lachesis.*
Belladonna	Headache, tongue bright red, strawberry appearance, pupils dilated delirium, throat burns like fire, feels raw, pain on swallowing, thirstless as fluids cause spasm.
Mercurius	The throat is hot and dry, speech is difficult, and the whole area is inflamed, infected and swollen. Swallowing is painful, and the temperature raised.
Aconite	Dryness, roughness, burning, hoarseness, after exposure to cold wind, acute high temperature, throat congested, eyes sparkling.
Baryta Carb	More tonsil infection and quinsy, sore throat develops slowly, glands swollen, pain on swallowing.
Dulcamara	There is a raw soreness, and burning pains, thick sticky saliva, and an aggravation with any change of atmospherics, or with cold and damp.
Hepar Sulph.	Very irritable, sense of fish-bone stuck in throat, worse from cold or draught.
Merc. Sol.	Foul tongue and mouth, thirst and salivation, yellow coating to tongue, throat feels dry, worse at night.
Lachesis	Starts on the left side, bluish colour to throat, can swallow solids better than fluids, and better for solid food, but intolerant of any pressure in the neck area.

Splinters

Definition   The presence of a fine piece of wood or metal in the skin where it acts as an irritant, and foreign body.

Causes   One of the commonest of household mishaps.

Symptoms   Pain, infection, swelling.

Treatment   *Ledum, Arnica* lotion.

Arnica   Apply lotion externally.

Ledum   The most useful remedy for any deep, circumscribed wounds, with infection, redness, and the local formation of pus. There is very commonly a sensation of cold and chill present in the patient, and a craving for heat and generalized warmth.

Sprains

Definition	The tendons and ligaments in the area are stretched, torn and over-extended.
Causes	Slipping, falling, acute trauma.
Symptoms	Pain, incapacity, tenderness, swelling, bruising.
Treatment	*Calcarea; Arnica; Bellis; Rhus Tox.; Bryonia; Ruta; Ledum.*
Calcarea	Indicated for the weak flabby, fat child. Chilly, and where particularly the ankles are weak, and twisting or sprain is common.
Arnica	For the shock and to allay the swelling, and lessen pain. Use both internally, and apply locally as a lotion.
Bellis	One of the most efficient and rapid remedies, relieving the swelling and the pain of stretched ligaments, and particularly indicated when the injury is on the left side of the body.
Rhus Tox.	When the sprain is due to a fall or injury, and there is pain and stiffness, and swelling, it should be given following *Arnica*. It may also be applied locally as the lotion.
Bryonia	If involving a joint which is painful and swollen.
Ruta	Often helpful, in sprains and injury to ligaments.
Ledum	Useful when there is severe bruising and haematoma. Either internally, or locally as the lotion.

Stammering

Definition   A spasmodic speech defect, worse at times, particularly under stress or with effort.

Causes   Unknown.

Symptoms   The characteristic speech defect.

Treatment   *Stramonium; Hyoscymus; Arsenicum; Zincum; Cuprum Met.; Agaricus.*

Stramonium   The face is often red, hot and sweaty, the person excitable, often unstable and imaginative, or deluded, the speech is erratic, irregular and unpredictable.

Hyoscymus   Indicated when the speech is over-hurried and out of rhythm and phase, so that there is an attempt to over-compensate by trying to catch-up which worsens the stammer.

Arsenicum   One of the most valuable of all remedies.

Zincum   General twitching is a feature, particularly of the limbs and feet, and this may also affect the tongue, so that speech is incoherent.

Cuprum Met.   Spasm is the great characteristic of the remedy in all areas of the body and the remedy is indicated when the stammer is spasmodic, and the speech heavy and laboured.

Agaricus   The person affected is particularly nervous, and tense, with marked tic-like movements, foolish, inappropriate behaviour. They are very sensitive to the cold, and the circulation is always poor, the extremities cold or blue.

Styes

Definition	A small localized infection of the hair follicle root on the edge of the eyelid.
Causes	Usually self-infected, from unconsciously rubbing the eyelid with the dominant hand, debility, impetigo. Personal hygiene is important.
Symptoms	Pain, redness, usually of the upper lids, there may be a discharge of pus or fluid matter, causing the lids to stick together in sleep. Lids may become crusty.
Treatment	*Pulsatilla; Sulphur; Aconite; Hepar Sulph.; Calcarea; Staphysagria.*
Pulsatilla	Usually adequate, and is the first remedy to give.
Sulphur	Of value if recurrent, untidy-looking, and the eyes are very red.
Aconite	Give early if there is fever, restlessness and acute pain.
Hepar Sulph.	Another very valuable remedy when *Pulsatilla* fails or is not indicated.
Calcarea	Of value if recurrent and fitting the *Calcarea* type.
Staphysagria	Usually of the lower lid, and with the characteristic extremely irritable temperament.

Teething

Definition	Pain, irritability, and discomfort, occurring in the young child with the eruption of the first teeth.
Causes	The natural process of dentition.
Symptoms	Swollen and tender gums, increased salivation, fever, irritation, crying, restlessness, sleep interrupted.
Treatment	*Chamomilla; Aconite; Colocynth; Belladonna; Nux Vomica; Calcarea.*
Chamomilla	Child irritable, one cheek pale the other flushed, diarrhoea.
Aconite	If feverish and if acute.
Colocynth	If colic is present.
Belladonna	Irritability, flushed cheeks, convulsions.
Nux Vomica	If constipation is present.
Calcarea	Teething delayed, slimy mucous diarrhoea.

Temperature

Definition A rise in temperature above 98.4°F (body heat) for practical purposes, although the individual varies slightly around this figure and is often slightly lower.

Causes An infection somewhere in the body, and more rarely, when causes are unknown, but not associated with infection, may be emotional.

Symptoms Heat, irritability, weakness, crying, no appetite, constipation.

Treatment *Aconite; Belladonna; Bryonia; Arsenicum; Nux Vomica; Rhus Tox.*

Aconite Due to dry cold wind or fear, restlessness, intense thirst, alternating chills and flushes, dry hot skin.

Belladonna Intense, violent redness of face, confusion, throbbing headache.

Bryonia Worse for movement, cough, yellow coated tongue, constipation, shooting pains, irritable.

Arsenicum If severe and prolonged, with prostration.

Nux Vomica When associated with acute coryza.

Rhus Tox. Pain, fever due to exposure to cold and damp.

Tonsillitis

Definition   Infection of the tonsils.

Causes   Throat or upper respiratory tract infection.

Symptoms   Pain, swelling of the throat, burning, fever, swallowing is painful, cervical glands enlarged and tender, earache.

Treatment   *Belladonna; Merc. Sol.; Hepar Sulph.; Baryta Carb.; Lachesis; Mercurius; Calc. Phos.*

Belladonna   Usually right sided, and very acute attacks with redness and swelling of the tonsillar area, fever. The neck is often stiff and inflamed. Pain is severe.

Merc. Sol.   There is a severely infected tonsil, with a painful and dry throat, often with a pustular discharge which may lead on to suppuration and quinsy, the pain is usually worsened by swallowing, or speech.

Hepar Sulph.   There is a purulent infection with splinter-like sensation in the throat, high temperature and shivering, with abscess formation.

Baryta Carb.   For milder recurrent cases often following exposure to cold or chill. The tonsils are very large and there is considerable cervical lymph gland enlargement which is often tender. The right tonsil is often affected and the typical *Baryta* child is somewhat timid and backward at school.

Lachesis   A remedy when the left tonsil is affected, and the tonsil is blue and swollen. The pain is worse on swallowing and taking hot drinks.

Mercurius   Another remedy when there is a severe purulent infection, often with ulcers, foetid breath, stinging throat pain and marked sweating with a temperature.

Calc. Phos.   For chronic cases in the *Calcarea* make-up. The tonsils are large, pale, inflamed. Hearing may be impaired.

Toothache

Definition   Acute or dull pain in the mouth, tooth, gum, sometimes radiating to the face, orbit and opposite jaw.

Causes   Dental caries or root abscess formation.

Symptoms   Dull ache, at time throbbing, with swelling of the face and jaw.

Treatment   *Aconite; Chamomilla; Silica; Plantago* locally and internally; *Arnica; Belladonna; Kreosote; Coffea; Merc. Sol.; Staphysagria.*

Aconite   When aggravated by cold wind, better for cold water, one-sided.

Chamomilla   Severe toothache, worse at night, and in a warm room. Irritability is marked, and may be a precipitating factor in triggering off the pain.

Silicea   The pain is aggravated by either hot or cold food, or cold air. Often worse at night, and commonly associated with a root abscess, or gum boil.

Plantago   Use locally and internally. Teeth sensitive to touch. Teeth feel too long.

Arnica   For pain after a filling and before-hand.

Belladonna   Stabbing, throbbing pain in the gums, often like migraine.

Kreosote   Foetid breath, constipation, caries.

Coffea   Relief with cold water is characteristic of the typical pain.

Merc. Sol.   Stabbing pains radiating to the ears, worse at night, profuse salivation.

Staphysagria   The pain is severe, the teeth especially sensitive, so that the least touch, or cold air, sets off the toothache, especially at night. The pain is often worse after food, and is typically drawing and tearing in character, the cheek often swollen and red.

Vaccination (Reactions to)

Definition   Vaccination of the child with the cow-pox serum, causing a local reaction and response.

Causes   The small-pox vaccination.

Symptoms   Pain, swelling, general malaise, fever.

Treatment   *Variolinum 200; Thuja.*

Variolinum   When there has been a severe reaction to small-pox vaccination.

Thuja   When the child or person has had a reaction to vaccination and has never been really well since.

Worms

Definition	Infection of the caecum and upper colon, by the Oxyuris vermicularis. Anaemia.
Causes	Infection by the Oxyuris, ¼ to 1 inch long, thread-like and white worm. Moves rapidly and contracts when touched. Eggs enter body on inadequately washed vegetables.
Symptoms	Itching anal irritation, worse evening, itching nose, variable appetite, ineffective frequent defaecation, irritability, insomnia, enuresis, restlessness.
Treatment	*Cina; Teucrium; Santonine; Urtica Urens; Calcarea; Sulphur.*
Cina	When boring at the nose-tip, dark areas under the eyes, restlessness, grinding of the teeth in sleep, itching of the anus, gripes, starting in sleep, calling out in sleep, nausea, or vomiting, hiccup, tendency to diarrhoea.
Teucrium	Where there is much rectal itching, irritability, and sleeplessness, giddiness.
Santonine	Useful generally in all varieties of worm infection.
Urtica Urens	For excessive night-time itching of the anus.
Calcarea	Often very useful in children in the *Calcarea* constitution.
Sulphur	For worm colic.

Wounds

Definition   Small usually clean wounds of the skin and sub-cutaneous tissue.

Causes   Trauma, or the bite of an animal.

Symptoms   Usually minimal, may be pain, tenderness, redness.

Treatment   *Hypericum* tincture; *Ledum.*

Hypericum tincture   This should be applied locally.

Ledum   In the sixth potency, this is the immediate and best remedy for a clean puncture wound of the skin.

2.

ILLNESSES DURING ADOLESCENCE

The acute and turbulent changes which are so characteristic of adolescence occur after the relatively calm period of the younger pre-adolescent child. Puberty marks the onset of adult sexuality with profound physiological, hormonal and psychological changes — sudden spurts of growth and weight, the development of body hair, and the onset of the menstrual cycle. All these changes may become the centre of attention and a preoccupation which is sometimes unhealthy, particularly if delayed at all. There are inevitably many comparisons with friends. When any of these changes are delayed, perhaps until the age of fourteen or fifteen, or when growth is slow and the teenager is small of stature for whatever reason, this may become a source of anxiety for the growing adolescent, who is particularly conscious of his or her body, and tends to measure acceptance by it.

During adolescence, sexuality reaches a maturity which is usually expressed indirectly. Much of the drive is channelled into physical activity, such as competitive sport, or creative expressions, such as art or ballet. All these activities are associated with great urgency, drive, enthusiasm, and impatience. Feelings are strong and characterized by a 'Why wait, let's do it now' attitude. The sexuality provides the underlying force and drive to the typical adolescent push and bravado. At the same time it is a source of much anxious preoccupation and intensity.

Some Examples of Homoeopathic Adolescent Temperamental Types

Some are especially sensitive and often precocious, both physically and mentally, seeming mature and older than their years. Inviting adult problems on youthful shoulders leads to their often worried expression and general concern and anxiety about the future. Generally they are very attractive, gifted, and charming. Although artistic, they tend to be somewhat over-intellectual, preoccupied with problems of world events, finance in the home, or the family generally. However, under this facade of maturity and social aplomb, they are highly nervous and lack confidence, covering this by their considerable ability and skill with words, and a plausible pseudo-adult manner. It is this type of temperament that responds so well to *Lycopodium*.

Another type of adolescent is artistic, but more passive, and obviously shy and moody, without the apparent maturity of the *Lycopodium* make-up. They look and feel like a young child, are easily influenced, changeable and lack the depth and ability of the former. There is a tendency to be solitary or in the company of a younger child, as opposed to the *Lycopodium* adolescent who is usually in the company of an adult. Often, they are too ready to please, tending to agree for the sake of peace and quiet, whatever the occasion. This over-compliant attitude undermines their confidence and the whole of their personality development. At other times they can be stubborn and difficult, as part of their general changeable tendency. Much reassurance and sympathy is needed. Girls often have difficult, delayed, or painful periods which are always a nuisance and a problem from the onset. This form of temperament responds well to *Pulsatilla*.

Others rebel, becoming the typical awkward teenager, defiant and difficult to handle. Fiery, over-sensitive and rebellious, any trivial remark may be taken as an insult or intended hurt. Frequently at variance with their parents or teachers, they often associate with a minority group, and may become violent or destructive within this group, although not usually directly within the family. Impatient, tending to get too quickly involved in issues, at the same time they easily feel misunderstood or rejected. They are passionately determined to take a stand, often on political or social issues, and may defiantly oppose authority in whatever area of injustice they are currently preoccupied. These social concerns and attitudes towards authority are an extension of similar attitudes to the boundaries and limits within the family, where they are often equally in a position of protestation and conflict. This type of temperament often shows qualities of strength and leadership, can be very loyal and a tower of strength to friends especially anyone regarded as being in any way 'hard done by' or the 'underdog'. A great weakness is their tendency to have a 'short fuse' and to over-react in any situation, rising up with spasms of righteous indignation and rage, even with friends, which makes them difficult, unpredictable and often unreliable. Colicky digestive troubles and constipation are the commonly associated physical problems. It is this behaviour pattern that is indicated for *Nux Vomica*.

Some adolescents are always in a mess and untidy, both in their physical appearance and in their mind and thinking. They are full of plans and projects, many of them ambitious, but often unfortunately unrealistic, changing and unlikely to be ever realized. Ideas may be thought about, planned and discussed for many months without ever coming to fruition. Often they are drop-outs, and unlikely to act with any organized or thought-out initiative, tending to follow the herd. Others are preoccupied with unreal pursuits and fantasies in a solitary way. Their physical weakness is the skin which tends to be chronically infected and unhealthy, with frequent crops of boils and spots, adding to their unhealthy and unattractive appearance. *Sulphur* is the remedy of choice for this type of adolescent behavioural pattern.

There is another type of irritable, surly adolescent, often tall and thin with a long back and sallow pale skin. They are never really well, always complaining and under the weather, exhausted and even wake up feeling tired. Frequently they are late for work or school and in trouble because of it and their attitudes of criticism and irritability. There is always an improvement with exercise, and the more energetic they are, the better they feel. Often they blossom in company, and once persuaded to mix socially, quickly forget their many ills. Girls are frequently incapacitated by heavy and painful menstrual periods with dragging down colicky pains and a general sense of misery. Constipation is a common problem as is back ache. *Sepia* is the remedy of choice for this type of adolescent.

Some adolescents turn into themselves and are solitary, varying in mood from angry and childish behaviour to tears and hysteria, being especially prone to emotional outbursts. They quickly become ill or upset at a change of routine, such as before an interview, an examination or perhaps a change of job or school. Difficult to help or relate to, they shun sympathy or consolation in any form, preferring to be alone. In general, they lack confidence and are never really natural or able to be themselves in any social situation, always seeming to be acting, distant and remote or uninvolved. There is frequently a great craving for salt, and they are commonly either better or worse for being at the sea-side. The remedy of choice for this temperament is *Natrum Mur*.

Because their identity and self-image is weak and lags behind external and physical maturity, the development of a secure identity is often not established until early adulthood, and for some even later. This makes the adolescent extremely vulnerable and suggestible, often needing to identify with whatever is being currently put out by the media as the current teenage ideal of health, success and potency. The adolescent deals with these basic problems by creating a temporary identity for himself, which ensures his acceptance by others of his peer-group. This identity affects every aspect of his individuality: the pattern of his clothes, taste in music, eating, smoking and drinking habits, and some may experiment with drugs and sexuality. The need to present an image of security, strength, and indifference to changes of climate, means that the adolescent rarely dresses warmly enough, and coughs and colds are depressingly frequent and prolonged.

At the same time as the physical changes of the adolescent, there is a recurrence of early childhood demands, with attention-seeking behaviour, including demands for the sweet foods usually associated with the younger child. Rich, starchy snack foods and drinks are all taken to excess, often compulsively with their own group. Meals are also rushed, irregular, often of poor quality, particularly those outside the home, when anything instant and quick is preferred. This poor diet, together with the deeper associated hormonal changes, accounts for many of the typical adolescent problems with general health.

Skin infections are very common, especially acne, styes, boils, eczema and dandruff. There is a high incidence of digestive problems, including stomach cramps, pains and diarrhoea, constipation, often wind and flatulence. Dental caries is also frequent, together with many chronic mouth and gum conditions, often aggravated by the low grade infection and smoking. Unfortunately the excess consumption of sweets and cigarettes fails to give the reassurance or sense of confidence and relaxation that is sought and, by undermining health, they create additional anxiety.

In some this may lead to an unhealthy preoccupation with self and body functions, especially when there is already a tendency to introspection and hypochondriasis. This may take the form of excessive dieting, sometimes leading to anorexia nervosa, especially when there is an underlying distorted body image. An anorexic illness may occur when a simple weight control programme has got out of hand and become compulsive and part of a mental illness. Profound hormonal and physiological changes occur as a result of the extreme weight loss and, in some cases, this may even endanger life if the disease is very severe. Powerful remedies which have a strong balancing effect upon the mental processes, such as *Natrum Mur.*, *Pulsatilla*, or *Argentum Nit.*, are often very helpful. The attitudes of the parents themselves is a key factor, and their understanding and general approach may affect the duration and outcome of the disease. Whenever possible, such obsessional tendencies should be checked and counteracted in the earliest stages by an open straightforward approach and discussion. Whenever there is a possible anorexic tendency, it should be dealt with before it becomes a psychological problem and a health hazard.

The ideal diet for the average adolescent is a varied one with a plentiful supply of raw foods, protein, and fresh fruit. In general starch and carbohydrates are best kept on the low side, because of the common tendency to starchy, snack-foods between meals.

All these adolescent difficulties can seem very bewildering to parents, unless they are in touch with the same struggles which they themselves went through at this stage with their own families. When a balanced overall position is taken, the often apparently outrageous, anti-social, non-caring attitudes which seem to lack any sense of respect or direction, can be put into proper focus. When seen as the struggles of the growing, bewildered young adult, desperately trying to find himself, a more positive and confident stance can be adapted, allowing the parents to remain calm and not unduly over-anxious, whatever the pressures. The knowledge that by the early adult years, most of these problems will have been resolved, can also convey to the adolescent some of the quiet calm and confidence that he is so desperately seeking.

SOME TYPICAL CASES

A student aged eighteen came to me because of recurrent sore throats and catarrh with a clear discharge over the past year. At times her throat became dry and hot, so that it was difficult to swallow. Over the past few months she had been more irritable and easily annoyed, although she was usually good-tempered. She was an out-going person, not particularly solitary, but felt somewhat nervous in crowds and lifts. She liked sunny weather, but not too hot, with a breeze. Her taste in foods was for sweets and chocolates and she took little salt or fat. She rarely cried, and was not often thirsty. She had a very dry skin and rarely sweated. *Lycopodium* was prescribed in high potency. A month later she was better generally, although still getting occasional sore throats. *Kali. Bich. 6* was given for a period of a month, when she felt much better and was free of all symptoms.

*   *   *

A boy of fifteen was seen because of his small size, and general failure to develop. He was also very short-sighted. Puberty had been very delayed, and pubic hair had only just developed over the past few months. His sight had been deteriorating over the past three to four years and he could hardly read what was written on the black-board at school. He was a nervous boy, frightened of the dark and a bed-wetter until a year before. He cried easily, was thirsty and rarely sweated. His favourite foods were savoury and he added a lot of salt to everything he ate. His birth weight had been normal and he was breast fed for nine months. He was given *Natrum Mur. 10M* and *Ruta 6*. Two months later there was a marked increase in sexual characteristics and he was beginning to put on weight. The eye fatigue was beginning to improve and he was generally feeling better.

*   *   *

An eighteen year old girl came because she was feeling low, worn-out and depressed since finishing her 'A'-level examinations two weeks previously. She felt dizzy, had a generalized pressure headache, and did not want to go out, feeling black, despairing and tense. She felt that something very serious was wrong with her, that perhaps she was dying, and she was always in floods of tears and unable to get off to sleep. She was not enjoying her food and had vague chest pains on breathing in. She was not particularly thirsty and could on no account tolerate heat. She was given *Pulsatilla 10M* and when seen two weeks later there was a marked improvement in her depression and general confidence. I have seen her from time to time over the past year and there has been no recurrence of the severe depression.

*   *   *

A girl of twelve came for help with facial acne and blackheads which had occurred on and off over the past two years. Otherwise she was quite well, apart from a tendency to get recurrent conjunctivitis and red eyes. She was rather reserved, quiet and shy, rather a loner, and had little to say for herself. She was untidy and left her things everywhere at home. She enjoyed all foods, particularly sweets, took a lot of salt, and quite liked cream and eggs. Generally she felt worse for cold damp weather, but quite liked the snow and mild warmth. She was given *Sulphur 10M* and seen a month later, when she reported the acne had improved and that she felt well. However, there was still some irritation present. Because of her placid make-up and warm sweaty hands she was prescribed *Calc. Sulph.* This led to a further improvement and a lessening of the irritation.

There was a student aged fifteen, brought by her mother because she had been away from school for a year and a term with school problems, and a history of panic attacks since the age of six. At that time — when in the junior school — she had suddenly felt frightened and not wanted to go to school (for no obvious reasons), but this had only lasted a few days. The onset of the panic was associated with a terror of swimming lessons. Over the past few years she had attended parties but was now going out less frequently. However, she liked people, disliked heights, lifts and the underground, and was generally neat and tidy in her habits. She was intolerant of heat and preferred the rain or being outside in the cool air. She was quite thirsty and enjoyed sweet foods, particularly chocolates. She was prescribed *Argentum Nit.* in high potency, and seen three weeks later when she reported feeling a lot better and more normal and that she had started leaving home and working in a tutors centre for two hours every day. A month later she was back full time at school, clinging a bit to her friends, but over the severe and paralyzing phobic episodes.

Acne

Definition   A chronic inflammation of the sebaceous glands of the skin, with the eruption of hard elevations, and areas of infection with redness.

Causes   Diet over-rich in carbohydrates, constitutional, lack of hygiene.

Symptoms   Discomfort, irritation, infection, discharge.

Treatment   *Kali. Brom.; Sulphur; Psorinum; Calc. Sulph.; Kali. Sulph.; Pulsatilla; Ant. Crud.; Arsenicum.*

Kali. Brom.   Very useful remedy in chronic acne, particularly on the face, neck and upper back.

Sulphur   One of the best remedies with raised hard circular areas which are red and often sore and infected. Usually they are worse for water.

Psorinum   Useful where there is a severely infected acne, often boils, and especially marked itching is a feature, leading to scratching and re-infection.

Calc. Sulph.   In a *Calcarea* make-up with pallor, sweaty forehead and flabbiness, this is very useful.

Kali. Sulph.   This remedy is very effective when there is the combined *Kali.* and *Sulphur* features of weakness and skin infections.

Pulsatilla   Helpful in all cases which are aggravated by heat. Usually they take a lot of starchy foods and are thirstless.

Ant. Crud.   There are multiple infected acne spots on the face and it is often associated with digestive upsets. The tongue has a white coating.

Arsenicum   Useful in chronic or severe cases when there is severe weakness associated.

Agoraphobia

Definition   The fear of going out from the security of the home alone.

Causes   Psychological, temperamental, familial.

Symptoms   Anxiety, fear at the need and thought of leaving the home alone. Usually they stay home, refuse to go out, or make excuses.

Treatment   *Argent. Nit.; Natrum Mur.; Gelsemium.*

Argent. Nit.   This is usually the most useful remedy when there is a strong phobic anxiety element present.

Natrum Mur.   This follows *Argent. Nit.* well once the immediate acute phobic situation has been dealt with.

Gelsemium   This has phobic anxiety symptoms less severe than *Argent. Nit.* and often a hysterical element is present.

Anorexia Nervosa

Definition   Loss of appetite, refusal to eat food, associated with a disturbed body image.

Causes   Profoundly psychological in a nervous sensitive withdrawn hypochondriacal person.

Symptoms   Obsessional preoccupation with dieting and weight loss; may hide food or deliberately regurgitate it; circulation often poor, greasy skin, acne, amenorrhoea.

Treatment   *Natrum Mur.; Silicea; Argent. Nit.* In all cases the diet must be adequate and well-balanced and the weight built up slowly.

Natrum Mur.   Is usually effective and helpful in most cases.

Silicea   Is useful in a thin pale chilly child, the extremities are usually cold and sweaty.

Argent. Nit.   Helpful when there is a phobic element present.

Bad Breath

Definition   Offensive foetid breath is complained of.

Causes   Decaying teeth gums or tonsils, excessive carbohydrates causing stasis or fermentation in the stomach.

Symptoms   The breath has an offensive putrid odour.

Treatment   *Nux Vomica; Mercurius; Carbo Veg.; Pulsatilla; Spigelia.*

Nux Vomica   Has offensive breath due to digestive upset or alcoholism. Usually they are irritable.

Mercurius   Has profuse offensive breath associated with much sweating of the body generally.

Carbo Veg.   Has flatulence, weakness, poor circulation, and particularly offensive breath, often from decaying teeth or infected gums.

Pulsatilla   There is offensive breath associated with indigestion. Like everything in the *Pulsatilla* make-up, the bad breath is also variable and changeable.

Spigelia   The breath is offensive and the tongue is coated white or yellow. Palpitations are commonly associated.

Black Eye

Definition   A symptom of trauma to the orbit, the discoloration, due to bruising and blood having seeped into the surrounding tissues from a ruptured blood vessel.

Causes   Always due to acute trauma to the orbit from a fall or a blow, and may be a symptom following concussion and fracture of the skull.

Symptoms   Pain, tenderness, swelling around the eye, which may be severe enough to obscure sight of the injured eye.

Treatment   *Arnica* lotion, applied locally, at an early stage; *Arnica* internally; *Hamamelis* lotion locally when the discoloration is more marked; *Ledum; Ruta.*

Arnica lotion   The remedy of choice for the typical bruising, swelling, and pain due to the subcutaneous haemorrhage into the subcutaneous tissues.

Arnica   It is also advisable to take the *Arnica* internally for a few days until the bruising and the swelling has subsided completely.

Hamamelis lotion   This remedy may be used locally to follow *Arnica*, if the area of redness and blueness has not completely gone after a few days. It has a specific action on all venous haemorrhages, and aids in their reabsorption.

Ledum   *Ledum* is another useful remedy for tender and painful hot swellings and can compliment *Arnica.*

Ruta   A useful eye remedy, and tonic. Use especially when there has been severe bruising of the surrounding muscles, and face.

Bleeding from Cuts and Wounds

Definition   Haemorrhage from traumatic causes.

Causes   Trauma.

Symptoms   Shock, bleeding, pallor, collapse.

Treatment   *Arnica; Calendula* tincture; *Hamamelis*. (The remedies should be given when the haemorrhage has been arrested. Stopping the flow of blood is always the first priority.)

Arnica   Should be given every fifteen minutes in 6 or 30c potency if there is arterial bleeding or collapse.

*Calendula   Apply locally when the haemorrhage is arterial. If
tincture*   severe, surgical ligation (tying up) may be required.

Hamamelis   Give internally in 6 potency and as a tincture locally — for venous bleeding (oozing).

Blushing

Definition   Sudden flushing spontaneously, of the cheeks, neck and face in an emotionally-charged situation.

Causes   Embarrassment; shyness; constitutional; immaturity; inexperience; over-protected child; familial.

Symptoms   Heat; redness; discomfort; embarrassment; shyness; may be sweating.

Treatment   *Phosphorus; Pulsatilla; Natrum Mur.; Ferrum Phos.*

Phosphorus   The adolescent is delicate, fine-boned and outgoing, but nervous, over-sensitive, and in constant need of reassurance. They flush up easily and often have a characteristic bead of sweat just above the upper lip.

Pulsatilla   This is one of the best remedies for blushing of emotional origin in a shy adolescent. They need reassurance, to be approved of, and attention. They easily burst into tears.

Natrum Mur.   Another useful remedy for nervous tense adolescents, unsure of themselves, ill at ease, and never quite able to relax and be natural in any social situation.

Ferrum Phos.   Another useful remedy with pallor and quick flushing in new or tense situations. They are somewhat less sensitive to external impressions than *Phosphorus*.

Body Odour

Definition   Offensive sweat and perspiration.

Causes   Constitutional, inadequate washing, and hygiene.

Symptoms   Odorous, often offensive, excessive sweating.

Treatment   *Nux Vomica; Calcarea; Silicea; Mercurius.*

Nux Vomica   Sweats profusely with exercise and emotion, and the sweat may be offensive.

Calcarea   Has a stale smelling sweat often on the hands and forehead.

Silicea   Has profuse sweating, particularly of the soles of the feet which may be offensive.

Mercurius   Has a very profuse offensive foetid sweat.

Boils

Definition	A suppurative swelling of the skin and subcutaneous tissues, usually hard, round, which may discharge.
Causes	Infection, usually circulatory, high blood sugar level, diabetes.
Symptoms	Pain, throbbing, redness, fever, glandular enlargement, may become a carbuncle.
Treatment	*Hepar Sulph.; Hypericum* tincture; *Silicea; Belladonna; Merc. Sol.; Sulphur; Tarentula.*
Hepar Sulph.	To mature the boil.
Hypericum tincture	Indicated when the area is particularly sensitive to touch, and the boil is in an area of the body where it affects the fine and peripheral nerves running over the swelling, and causing intolerable pain.
Silicea	If slow to mature, or chronic.
Belladonna	Painful, hot, shining, inflamed base, about to suppurate, before pus forms.
Merc. Sol.	Threatens to become putrid and suppurate.
Sulphur	To prevent recurrence.
Tarentula	Very acute, severe pain, stinging and throbbing.

Bruises

Definition   Damage to the surface of the body, without damaging the skin, but rupturing subcutaneous blood vessels, with bleeding into surrounding tissues.

Causes   Nearly always traumatic, but rarely spontaneous, when the blood clotting time is low.

Symptoms   Pain, swelling, discolouration locally.

Treatment   *Arnica; Conium; Ruta; Bellis; Symphytum* (shins); *Hamamelis.*

Arnica   Lotion locally, and internally.

Conium   If of the female breast.

Ruta   If it involves the periosteum (the fibro-vascular layer which envelopes the bones).

Bellis   A very useful remedy, particularly when the underlying tendons are affected, and there is pain, exhaustion, and weakness in the area.

Symphytum   Indicated when the blow has been to the shin, and involved the delicate periosteal covering of the bones, causing severe pain, and bruising to bone.

Hamamelis   After *Arnica* if ineffective.

Burns

Definition	Skin and subcutaneous injury, due to the effects of radiant or direct heat upon the area affected.
Causes	Excessive exposure to sun; electric fire/iron; scalds.
Symptoms	Pain, redness, blister formation, congestion, infection.
Treatment	*Cantharis; Urtica; Sulphur; Arnica; Hypericum.* Unless the burn is very mild, it should be treated by a physician.
Cantharis	For the pain, particularly when there is the formation of vesicle blisters, and burning pains, with the skin red, and peeling.
Urtica	Locally and internally, when less severe than the *Cantharis* severe burn, but where vesicle formation, and swelling is marked.
Sulphur	Indicated for mild scalds and burns, of small localized nature, and bright red, scarlet, swollen skin reaction. Usually follows *Cantharis.*
Arnica	For shock, when severe. There may be collapse and kidney failure, and urgent hospitalization must be considered. The patient must be kept warm and covered. Hot drinks may be needed if chilled.
Hypericum	Locally, except in very severe cases, when it is best avoided, and the burns kept covered by clean sheets, until hospital treatment can be organized in a special burns unit.

Cuts

Definition	Damage to the skin and, if deep, underlying muscle.
Causes	Always traumatic.
Symptoms	Pain and bleeding.
Treatment	*Calendula* lotion; *Hepar Sulph.; Silica; Hypericum; Arnica; Aconite; Belladonna.*
Calendula	Apply lotion locally.
Hepar Sulph.	If infected and suppurative.
Silica	When there is an unhealthy purulent discharge.
Hypericum	When infected.
Arnica	If there is shock.
Aconite	If painful and hot.
Belladonna	If painful, red and swollen, with temperature and headache.

Dandruff

Definition   A superficial skin affection with flaking off in scales, without discharge, usually of the scalp, rarely of the eyelids.

Causes   Constitutional, usually associated with a dry skin generally. It is sometimes allergic.

Symptoms   Dryness and itching; there may be redness and a sense of local heat.

Treatment   *Sulphur; Calc. Carb.; Sepia; Lycopodium; Arsenicum.* Wash hair with plain soap.

Sulphur   Helpful generally, particularly when there is associated acne, flaking and itching.

Calc. Carb.   Often helpful in certain *Calcarea* cases. Usually they tend to sweat across the forehead at night.

Sepia   Useful and often associated with dark brown patches and discolourations of the skin.

Lycopodium   This remedy is very helpful, particularly when there is a lot of flaking and scaling and a very dry skin.

Arsenicum   Useful as a hair tonic and when there is a dry flaking skin condition. They are always chilly and exhausted.

Delayed Puberty

Definition   Failure to develop the secondary sexual characteristics, of pubic hair, breast and menses, at the time expected for the particular person.

Causes   Delayed development; may be small in height; may be familial.

Symptoms   As above.

Treatment   *Baryta Carb.; Sabal Serr.; Silicea; Calcarea.* It is always initially helpful in these cases to give the constitutional remedy in high potency as a stimulus to normal development.

Baryta Carb.   This is a useful remedy for immature and delayed development.

Sabal Serr.   Helpful when the breast development is inadequate and retarded.

Silicea   This remedy can be very helpful in small, slender, fair haired adolescents with poor peripheral circulation, chilly, and profuse sweating of the extremities.

Calcarea   Helpful when the make-up is predominantly *Calcarea* in type. Usually all the milestones have been late or delayed throughout childhood.

Dental Haemorrhage

Definition   Haemorrhage during or following tooth extraction.

Causes   The dental extraction or treatment, rarely haemophilia or blood dyscrasia.

Symptoms   Bleeding, swallowing clots that may be afterwards vomited.

Treatment   *Calendula* tincture; *Phosphorus; Arnica; Hamamelis* tincture. Packing and local pressure and treatment. Should the haemorrhage fail to stop, then hospitalization may be required.

Calendula tincture Apply locally, pack socket if necessary with cotton wool or thin gauze strip soaked in *Calendula*.

Hamamelis tincture   This is useful for venous oozing after dental extraction, apply locally as for *Calendula*.

Phosphorus   When there is oozing of bright red blood.

Arnica   Helpful generally for shock and weakness.

Depression

Definition   Depressive symptoms in adolescents.

Causes   Psychological in a sensitive child, may be familial or constitutional.

Symptoms   Anxiety, lack of confidence, insomnia, no appetite, lethargic, no interests, apathetic, withdrawn, solitary, weeping.

Treatment   *Medusa; Lycopodium; Natrum Mur.; Pulsatilla; Argent. Nit.*

Medusa   This is one of the best remedies for adolescent depression.

Lycopodium   This is indicated in a forgetful rather hypochondriacal child, that rarely sweats, is timid and tends to crave sweet foods.

Natrum Mur.   This is helpful in the more remote solitary nervous child, that shuns company and is usually a salt lover.

Pulsatilla   Indicated for the more changeable, emotionally unstable child with a tearful depression and disposition.

Argent. Nit.   This may be required when there is a phobic component and intolerance of heat.

Exam Fears

Definition   The phobia of taking examinations.

Causes   Shy; immaturity; lacks confidence; psychological and
                     may be familial.

Symptoms   Panic, anxiety, tension, pains anywhere in the body,
                     weeping, regressed behaviour with childish demands.

Treatment   *Argent. Nit.; Gelsemium.*

Argent. Nit.   This is the most useful and basic remedy, particularly
                     when there is an associated intolerance of heat and
                     digestive disorders such as flatulence.

Gelsemium   Another useful remedy, but usually secondary to *Argent.
                     Nit.* Usually they are weak, and collapsing at the knees
                     from panic.

Grazed Knee

Definition   Damage to the skin as from a fall, the main injury at a
superficial level and not involving deeper tissues.

Causes   Traumatic.

Symptoms   Pain, smarting, bruising, superficial bleeding.

Treatment   *Hypericum* tincture; *Hypericum; Arnica.* The area must
be thoroughly cleaned and any foreign particles
removed.

Hypericum   Apply locally and cover with a clean, preferably sterile,
tincture   dressing.

Hypericum   This may be taken twice daily for three days.

Arnica   Useful for shock and bruising, or blueness of the area.

Greasy Hair

Definition   The chronic or recurrent condition of lank, greasy hair.

Causes   Dietary, excessive carbohydrate intake; constitutional; lack of personal hygiene.

Symptoms   As above, often associated with a waxy unhealthy skin, and acne.

Treatment   *Thuja; Kali. Sulph.; Pulsatilla; Lycopodium.* More balanced life and diet, washing hair with plain soap.

Thuja   Useful general remedy for the condition.

Kali. Sulph.   This can often clear up the condition completely.

Pulsatilla   Helpful when the condition is worse before the period.

Lycopodium   This is often a useful remedy in dull, greasy, lifeless hair.

Grumbling Appendix

Definition   Pain in the lower abdomen, usually with associated tenderness, over the appendix area.

Causes   Sub-acute appendicitis, abdominal lymph adenopathy, spasm, constipation.

Symptoms   Pain, tenderness in the right lower abdomen without fever, usually.

Treatment   *Lachesis; Apis; Arsenicum; Bryonia; Rhus Tox.*
A surgical opinion may be required.

Lachesis   The pain is cutting in character, worse on waking, in the lower right abdominal quadrant.

Apis   The pain is stinging or burning, may occur after vaccination.

Arsenicum   The pain is burning in character, the patient is restless, anxious, thirsty for small sips of water; chill and exhaustion is marked. The tongue is red and uncoated.

Bryonia   The patient lies motionless and the least movement or jar aggravates the pain.

Rhus Tox.   The patient is restless, and is on the whole better for movement and warmth.

Hiccups

Definition	Brief spasmodic contractions of the diaphragm.
Causes	Indigestion.
Symptoms	The typical spasm and hiccup noise, lasting for a few minutes usually.
Treatment	*Nux Vomica;* Ginseng tincture; *Cyclamen; Ignatia; Cicuta; Mercurius.*
Nux Vomica	When the condition occurs before meals.
Ginseng tincture	One of the most useful remedies in all forms of hiccup.
Cyclamen	When associated with breathing distress, and better after taking water.
Ignatia	When the hiccup is loud and noisy.
Mercurius	When the hiccup is worse for drinking water.

Menstruation (Delayed Onset)

Definition	When the normal twenty-eight-day cycle has not commenced by the age of fourteen years.
Causes	Constitutional, anaemia, stress and nervousness, imperforate hymen.
Symptoms	Failure to establish a regular cycle, having once appeared, or totally without appearance at all.
Treatment	*Baryta Carb.; Bryonia; Pulsatilla; Veratum Alb.; Sepia; Aconite; Natrum Mur.; Sulphur; Cimicifuga.*
Baryta Carb.	Indicated for periods where the onset is delayed, or of a very brief duration.
Bryonia	If vicarious nose-bleeding occurs.
Pulsatilla	Pain in the abdomen and back, headache and nausea, anaemia, palpitation.
Veratum Alb.	The onset is suppressed and often associated with shivering, nausea, vomiting and diarrhoea.
Sepia	If leucorrhoea is present.
Aconite	Suppressed from chill or fright.
Natrum Mur.	Constipation, chilliness, anaemia, thin woman.
Sulphur	Pain in abdomen and loins, vertigo, throbbing head, constipation.
Cimicifuga	Headache, insomnia, pain in left breast.

Shyness

Definition   Excessive self-awareness, lack of confidence, and a tendency to withdraw from the limelight.

Causes   Temperamental. Often familial in origin.

Symptoms   Embarrassment, discomfort, awkwardness, blushing, timidity, worse in any new or unexpected or unfamiliar situation.

Treatment   The person's constitutional remedy; *Lycopodium; Argent. Nit.; Natrum Mur.; Pulsatilla.*

Lycopodium   Helpful when the person likes their own company, but needs people to be in the house and not too far away. Generally they are rather shy and unsure of themselves — but respond well to encouragement and reassurance.

Argent. Nit.   Useful when there is a phobic element and always worse in heat.

Natrum Mur.   Much more solitary and independent than *Lycopodium*, they are always nervous and unsure of themselves in any social situation and never really able to completely relate or join in what is going on.

Pulsatilla   The shy, fair, timid agreeable, placid person, anxious to please, weeps easily and in need of company and re-assurance that she is liked and popular. Can change from shyness to obstinate stubbornness very quickly. Worse in a hot room, and needs an open window or cool spot.

Travel Sickness

Definition	Nausea and vomiting occurring when travelling, either by sea, air, or car.
Causes	Constitutional, reading when in a car, suggestion, emotional.
Symptoms	Pallor, nausea, sweating, retching, dizziness, fainting, weakness, prostration.
Treatment	*Cocculus; Nux Vomica; Petroleum; Tabacum; Kreosotum; Borax; Rhus Tox.*
Cocculus	Salivation, worse for smell of food, better for lying down.
Nux Vomica	Associated with constipation and indigestion. Splitting headache.
Petroleum	Nausea, vomiting, giddiness. Water accumulates in mouth. Better for eating during attack, worse sitting-up, bright light.
Tabacum	Indicated where there is weakness, sweating, nausea, trembling.
Kreosotum	The main indication is of nausea, vomiting, retching, burning pains, thirst is marked, and the limbs are often chilled. Restlessness.
Borax	(Air travel) worse from downward motion, air pockets.
Rhus Tox.	There is severe nausea, restlessness, improved by lying down.

Whitlow

Definition   A localized, suppurative, infection, at the end of the finger, or the sides of the nail.

Causes   Cut or injury, often trivial, introduces infection, recurrent.

Symptoms   Throbbing pain, heat, purulent discharge, nail may be elevated, or fall off, the infection may travel up the arm, involve the bone and axillary glands.

Treatment   *Silicea; Belladonna; Mercurius; Hepar Sulph.; Lachesis; Arsenicum.*

Silicea   The 'mother of pus' remedy of the old homoeopaths, and indicated whenever there is a condition of a non-acute localized purulent state. *Silicea* will slowly and thoroughly clean out and naturally drain the area.

Belladonna   If much inflammation and fever.

Mercurius   Indicated for an acute tender painful infection, where there are painful glands in the arm-pit, or infection of the lymphatics with red streaks along the arm.

Hepar Sulph.   When there is severe infection.

Lachesis   If finger bluish.

Arsenicum   Burning pain, finger is blackish, prostration.

3.

ACUTE ILLNESSES OF ADULT COUPLES

This can be one of the most active and pressured periods of life. Couples are busily involved and preoccupied with the basic needs of the family. Buying a house, negotiating a mortgage, locating schools and planning for their future life together leave little time for rest and leisure. Yet this is also a time when people experience an overwhelming sense of physical and mental well-being.

After the turbulence of adolescence the young couple have the possibility of a better relationship with their parents on a more equal footing. Many of the frustrations and earlier difficulties of the teenage years have lessened, and a more mutually supportive friendly contact can be established, with visits something to look forward to. Naturally this varies with individual temperaments and tolerance levels and with the patterns of earlier relationships.

Most couples experience a sense of buoyant health and energy, reflected by feelings of elation and vitality, and a sense of achievement. There is often a sense of invulnerability, as energy, fed by peak sexual drives, gives an added sense of power and strength. Although there is little time to pause and think, it seems impossible that any health problems could occur to check the flow of seemingly boundless energy. Yet even the apparently healthy young couple can develop mild and short-lived illnesses, and they are not immune from the severe viral infections which may cause such serious illnesses as meningitis or broncho-pneumonia. It is often after such severe illness that the myth of adolescent invulnerability is put to the test and finally snapped, leading to more adult and mature attitudes.

Often couples are needed to support other members of the family. The common mishaps and infections of their own children require care and reassurance, and when there are parents or grandparents living nearby, help may also be required by them.

Many first-aid problems occur with accidents involving ladders, power tools, mechanical equipment and in the pursuit of sport. Minor injuries quickly respond to such first-aid remedies as *Arnica*, *Calendula*, *Hypericum*, and *Bellis Perennis*. Extensive lacerations, infected wounds, or severe burns require hospital treatment and specialist advice.

Hay fever, catarrh and recurrent sore throats can involve the parents as well as the children, in the continuation of a childhood or adolescent problem. All these conditions are aggravated by central heating in the office or at home. In over-heated modern buildings, the use of a humidifier and setting the bedroom thermostat several degrees lower than in the lounge is beneficial. There is usually a good response to such recommended remedies as *Pulsatilla*, *Kali. Carb.*, *Phytolacca* and *Sulphur*.

Coughs and colds are common in adults, particularly when under strain. Severe infection can lead to chest complications such as asthma, bronchitis or pneumonia. In a heavy smoker, following a spate of late nights or increased work pressure, the young adult can quite suddenly become acutely ill and laid low with little warning other than minor fatigue and loss of energy. When there is an acute chest infection bed rest is necessary and the classic lung remedies of *Bryonia*, *Phosphorus*, *Ant. Tart.*, and *Spongia*, can stimulate a rapid return to health.

Digestive attacks occur from either dietary indiscretions or infection. The majority of such problems are of a temporary nature, commonly occurring after a period of indulgence or change of eating habits. There is a positive response to *Nux Vomica*, *Carbo Veg.*, *Lycopodium*, *Arg. Nit.*, and *Pulsatilla*.

The over-intense young adult, living on hurried pre-packed meals, may eventually develop a gastric or duodenal ulcer. The main symptoms are of pain with discomfort and nausea after meals, temporarily relieved by eating. Frequently the problem is long-standing with a family tendency to digestive disorders, and a flare-up may follow a period of undue emotional strain. Because meals need to be small, regular and carefully prepared during treatment, social life and enjoyment can become restricted. This may lead to further limitations and frustration. The whole approach to work and other commitments needs careful reconsideration and thought. When this is combined with the appropriate remedy such as *Kali. Carb*, *Ornithogalum*, or *Nux Vomica*, there should be a healing response.

Attacks of diarrhoea and food poisoning can involve the whole family. Most are short-lived and only a danger to the young baby because of the risks of dehydration. Colitis is a much more serious problem occurring from childhood onwards. Here there is a recurrent diarrhoea often containing mucus and blood, which may continue over many years and, when severe, causes weakness and collapse. In a colitis patient, the basic personality has a tendency to retain and bottle up, until intolerable tensions are experienced. Such tensions may then be expressed in short-lived outbursts of rage and tears; although with some, even with great provocation, such feelings are pushed down further and totally unexpressed. The disease is a handicap, and severe long-standing cases sometimes require major surgery. The response to homoeopathy is positive, and *Podophyllum* or *Phosphoric Acid* are particularly helpful. Because colitis is a potentially dangerous condition, it is not suitable for treatment by the family and, at least in the acute phase, should be cared for by the physician.

Constipation is common and may be long-standing, particularly in women, often developing during pregnancy. It is aggravated by allowing insufficient time for regular meals and exercise, when life is hurried and under pressure. Sensitivity to aluminium is a frequent cause, particularly when aluminium cooking utensils have been used over a long period, and it is usual also to see an atypical eczema and itchy eyes associated with this type of constipation. Homoeopathic aluminium in the form of *Alumina* is curative, but in all cases it is important to stop the use of laxatives and artificial remedies in order to encourage a return to normal bowel functioning. The use of added fibre in the form of bran is recommended to add extra bulk to the stool — a tablespoonful being sufficient in most cases. Depending upon the pattern of evacuation and the type of constipation, *Nux Vomica*, or *Bryonia* should give relief. When the problem is long-standing, the period of bowel retraining may take several months before the condition is finally cured.

Mild rheumatism is not uncommon in this age group, particularly following a sudden damp or cold spell. However, acute inflammatory arthritis is a severe crippling disease more common in young women than in men. Frequently there are underlying personality problems with unexpressed feelings of rage, frustration and resentment kept strictly under control with every other aspect of the personality. This is another illness best treated by the doctor during the acute phase. The most useful remedies include *Medorrhinum*, *Belladonna*, *Rhus Tox.*, *Staphysagria* and *Causticum*.

Many of the acute common infections of childhood also occur in adults, for example, mumps, which may follow contact with an infected child or be an isolated, sporadic case. Compared with the much more trivial childhood disease, the adult form is frequently more severe, with high fever, glandular involvement and exhaustion. The risk of complication can be totally reduced or avoided by using the specific mumps nosode. This is the homoeopathic equivalent to a specific mumps vaccine.

Chicken-pox in its infant form is not very common, but may occur in its more severe adult form as shingles. Superficial nerves are infiltrated by the virus, and the typical rash develops with pain, blistering and ulceration. There is a positive response to *Varicella* or chicken-pox nosode.

German measles is most dangerous in the early weeks of pregnancy, and contact should be avoided. If there is any risk, either by contact or because of an epidemic, the specific German measles nosode is recommended. Glandular fever may be a long drawn out illness requiring a lengthy period of convalescence. A combination of the specific nosode and the appropriate remedy for individual symptoms as they occur stimulates healing.

The menstrual periods may be painful or irregular for many reasons. Often there has been a problem since the early teens, and no regular rhythm established. Disturbances may occur as a complication of the contraceptive method used, and either the coil or the 'pill' can provoke problems. In all cases, professional advice, an examination, and proper diagnosis of the underlying cause, is recommended before beginning treatment. Some women from their late thirties onwards experience the onset of an early change, particularly when the periods began early. For irregular periods or menopausal problems, there is a rapid response to such remedies as *Pulsatilla, Sepia, Lachesis, Calcarea* and *Sabadilla*.

Piles and varicose veins are a frequent complication of childbirth, often associated with constipation. Attention to diet is important, and exercise such as walking or swimming helps to prevent a sluggish circulation. *Aesculus, Hamamelis,* and *Carbo Veg.* give a positive response in most cases.

During pregnancy there may be a threat of miscarriage, when a period of rest and specialist advice is required. The response to *Veratum Alb.* is often specific and stabilizes the pregnant uterus. For problems of infertility *Silicea* is of value, and is best given together with the constitutional remedy for the individual. In order to allow fertility to be maintained at an optimum level, it is always essential to improve the general health of the couple. When there is a mechanical problem, perhaps adhesions in the Fallopian tubes, surgical or other treatments may be combined with the homoeopathic remedy. During pregnancy, many women instinctively avoid anything harmful to the developing foetus, losing the taste for cigarettes and coffee. Others seem quite unaware of the dangers and are insensitive to the health risks for mother and baby.

Many mothers prefer to breast-feed their babies, stimulating a healthy child and a mother who feels more psychologically fulfilled. Breast-feeding is a natural process, and encourages strong feelings of closeness and attachment to the infant. Should difficulties occur, there is a rapid response to the homoeopathic remedy. For the majority, however, problems are few and only rarely does a breast become infected or an abscess develop, when *Belladonna* is curative.

A second pregnancy has important psychological implications for the family. It is particularly important to prepare the vulnerable first child at an early stage and by always sharing the excitement and planning, a sense of trust and participation is encouraged. This reinforces the child's own natural self-confidence and is a strong indication of the parent's love and affection which is particularly needed at this time. During further pregnancies, all the children should be encouraged to feel they have a part to play. The importance of the individual child should be stressed at all times together with the joy of extending the family as a shared experience. During the final weeks of pregnancy, *Caulophyllum* is valuable to ensure a smooth and uneventful delivery, stimulating uterine tone to the optimum.

It is not uncommon for a couple to experience a loss of sexual interest at some time during the relationship. For many complex reasons there is a natural variation and rhythm in the strength of desire, which is perfectly natural and normal. Friendly openness keeps anxiety about such fluctuations to a minimum and avoids a 'problem' developing due to misunderstanding or fear. In this way, a period of apparent impotency or frigidity need only be of passing significance when dealt with in a straightforward reassuring way. Naturally, an insensitive, aggressive or clumsy approach can equally convert a natural fluctuation into a fixed pattern of sexual difficulty. When the appropriate remedy is combined with a sensitive approach by both partners, there is a rapid return to normal.

Obesity puts a strain upon the heart and circulation, and is one of the major causes of disease in our time. It lessens the general efficiency of the heart and vital organs and is an important factor in the development of diabetes, gall-bladder disease, blood pressure and thyroid problems. The extra body weight also slows the ability to react to any traffic emergency and increases the dangers of road accidents, now one of the commonest causes of mortality.

High blood pressure, or hypertension, can occur in any age group, often following a period of stress and strain. It is a danger in the overweight, overworked person who takes little exercise and neglects the proper dietary and psychological needs of the body. Blood pressure is best treated by sensible prevention and must be taken seriously whenever it is diagnosed. If obesity is a factor then a carefully controlled reducing diet is essential. In a slim person, diet is less important and correct prescribing is the key to treatment. The most important remedies include *Natrum Mur.*, *Lycopus*, *Spartium*, and *Crataegus*. However, because of the dangers of side effects, hypertension is best treated by the physician.

Heart attacks are increasingly common in the young adult and usually follow a lengthy period of emotional and physical strain. In all cases it is necessary to re-think the lifestyle and priorities as soon as convalescence is over. Problems of finance and work should take second place to the urgent need of learning how to cope in a relaxed way with the many inevitable stresses and strains of modern living. A regular, rhythmic life is ideal, avoiding long periods of mental and physical fatigue, combined with a programme of regular exercise and a healthy balanced diet. Following an operation, acute illness or after a prolonged period of dieting or fasting, the body is nearly always weak, and reserves low. It is particularly unwise to overstrain the system at this time or when there are any additional tensions. This includes the run-up period to a much overdue annual holiday when many people work long extra hours at a time when they are already in need of a break.

It is not uncommon for an illness to occur when on holiday, and a recurrence of a chronic back problem, or a severe cold or flu are all frequent. For all of us regular breaks are necessary for health, but a change can be something quite simple — perhaps a quiet evening at home or a weekend away from time to time. The traditional holiday in cramped tiring conditions and oppressive heat can undermine health rather than improve it. The priority should always be an escape from routine thinking, particularly involving work and worry; and by lessening unhealthy attitudes, the soil of much chronic ill health can be improved.

Many people enjoy warmth and the sun for long hours without fatigue or harm. Others, particularly of the *Pulsatilla* make-up, are very sensitive to heat and suffer from it. For most people, excessive heat, and direct exposure is harmful, especially when they are in an anaemic or debilitated state. Severe burns, sunstroke, headache and cardiac collapse can all occur as complications of direct exposure to the sun's rays.

Many diseases of our present society are the result of intolerable pressures and competitive drives. It is increasingly commonplace to see couples working unnecessarily long hours without proper rest in a job that gives little satisfaction or promotion prospects. Work is often remote from home and the local community, requiring a tiring commuter journey in rush hour conditions, and the increasing difficulties of redundancy, take-over and general lack of available work in many areas adds to the problems. All these pressures and tensions, combined with an unhealthy diet and lack of creative leisure, contribute to a disturbing level of sickness and absenteeism. This is clearly reflected by the ever-increasing problems of depression, migraine, gall stones, blood pressure, insomnia and marital breakdown, seen in every doctor's surgery. A further complication is the demand for palliative drugs which often have powerful side reactions.

Many illnesses could be prevented by paying more attention to simple hygiene and the quality of diet and food in general. Tinned and instant foods should be kept to a minimum, particularly those containing harmful additives, preservatives and colorants. The excessive intake of sweet foods can be weakening and addictive and stimulate a hypoglycaemic or low blood sugar reaction in some people, causing recurrent weakness and collapse. Similarly the addition of large amounts of salt, whether natural sea salt or not, may be harmful to health. This compulsive, addictive intake of certain foods is of value in completing the homoeopathic picture of the individual and is an important guide to prescribing. Excesses of any kind are always harmful as they make demands upon the valuable reserves of the body which may require several months to be replenished. Sudden vigorous exercise which is not part of a planned training programme may be harmful; and the strain of nursing a sick relative or friend, or of working long hours without a break, can also take a heavy toll. When reserves are low, homoeopathic *China, Ferrum Phos., Phosphorus* or *Arnica* help restore a return to normal levels.

For many people, alcohol in moderate amounts is a stimulant, easing a social situation and having a pleasant tonic effect. However, like anything else taken to excess, it is also a poison and can severely inhibit the nervous system and damage other organs. Unless taken in sensible moderation, the drink habit is a frequent cause of depression and hardship, often provoking a great deal of unhappiness. Many illnesses could be avoided if consumption were more moderate. Excessive alcohol intake is an important cause of obesity, increasing the level of circulating fats in the bloodstream, and adding to the risk of coronary disease and hypertension. Whenever alcohol is a problem, it should be carefully discussed together to see if the causes of the excessive intake can be avoided on future occasions. Work tensions and certain occupations often add to the opportunities for drinking, making the problem more difficult to control and treat. Because alcohol has such a detrimental effect on judgement and thinking, its consumption adds to the difficulty of finding a reasoned, logical approach to curing it. *Nux Vomica*, is often helpful in reducing underlying tensions, but frequently the cure can only come from a combination of patient support and understanding, and a determined effort of will, based on the knowledge of the damage it is causing.

Many young people are cutting down, or stopping smoking altogether, sensing the addictive nature of the habit. It is often a psychological prop, and like most props tends to undermine and weaken, rather than strengthen. For any woman taking the 'pill', cigarette smoking is an additional danger, but especially when she is over the age of thirty, when the risks of serious circulatory side effects are increased. If there is any tendency at all to chronic chest problems, particularly asthma or bronchitis, it is wise to reduce consumption. Similarly, before an operation and during convalescence, the intake should cease altogether. Many cases of hernia and chronic backache are aggravated by smoker's cough, and it is a significant factor in many cases of lung cancer, and heart disease. Smoking can also provoke complications during pregnancy, with a significantly smaller baby at birth. There may also be complications during delivery, and often the vital feeding placenta and umbilical cord are less well developed.

Many couples now realize that the prolonged and repetitive use of drugs, particularly of the tranquilizer, anti-depressant, sedative and steroid type, is undesirable. Symptoms are often relieved for a time, but the underlying disease is unchanged or masked, and often pursues a more chronic course afterwards. Many of these drugs are severely addictive and, because of their side effects, create more problems than the original disease. As they act by suppressing or pushing the original disease deeper into the body, there are often reactions of fatigue or malaise. A true picture and expression of the basic illness does not occur, and the natural healing response is weak and undermined, so that an accurate homoeopathic diagnosis is not easily made. In a similar way, unless there are definite medical indications the prolonged and indiscriminate use of vitamins and appetite suppressants is unwise. In any case, haphazard self prescribing is never recommended.

Individual temperamental differences can create difficulties for the couple and homoeopathy is often helpful in treating them. *Lycopodium* is often indicated for those who leave everything to the last minute, particularly where there is a marked sense of insecurity. These people leave appointments and business arrangements as long as possible — there is a dread of commitments, of being organized or pressurized. With a more fussy personality, fidgety and over-controlled, the remedy of choice is frequently *Arsenicum*. Over-efficiency coupled with an inability to delegate, and a marked sense of irritability and pressure, even on holiday, indicates *Nux Vomica* as the remedy.

Because of the limitations of our pressurized society, some degree of depression, tension and loss of confidence is inevitable at times for everyone. A definite depressive tension state or phobic illness only tends to develop when there has been a breakdown in the very basic human needs of communication, understanding, trust and confidence. When there is a sense of isolation and an inability to share worries as they occur, there is always a danger that such fears become more severe and develop into symptoms of an illness. A good, sharing relationship allows such problems to be discussed in a straightforward natural way, putting potential fears and anxieties into perspective.

Severe mental problems are the province of the specialist, particularly when there is any tendency to manic excitement and delusional disturbances. During a particularly disturbed or violent phase, a period of rest in a hospital or clinic is usually required. In a severe problem, explorative psychotherapy is frequently helpful to ensure that underlying problems are brought to the surface. Specialized help may also be required when there is an emotional trauma perhaps following a physical assault, a period of acute grief, or when an acute accident with mutilating injury produces a state of shock. In general, having diagnosed the cause of the mental disturbance, with a sensible open approach by the family, there is often a very positive response to homoeopathic remedies. When there is a good background relationship within the family, patient support and trust, many such traumas do not take permanent root. The most valuable remedies in relieving the tensions and stresses of the disturbed mind are *Natrum Mur.*, *Lycopodium*, *Pulsatilla*, *Gelsemium*, *Ignatia* and *Nux Vomica*. For such problems, they must be prescribed in high potency by the physician.

All couples need to listen to each other, avoiding the temptation of reaching immediate conclusions about the motivations and intentions of the other. It is quite unrealistic to expect each other to behave in a logical consistent manner all the time. It is of course perfectly normal for men and women to be both rhythmic and variable, and understanding this is basic to any relationship. Attempts to impose a system of rigid behaviour patterns upon another is likely to fail and lead to further misunderstanding. Such demands are often little more than thinly disguised attempts to impose familiar patterns of reassurance, rooted in the past, which have nothing to offer either partner in terms of mutual growth and understanding. Such attitudes are damaging, and either partner can become trapped, lonely and isolated, and unable to express adequately either love or hate. Careful listening avoids these pitfalls and helps combat the dangers of misunderstanding and alienation. With patience, changes in attitudes are able to occur, however difficult and frightening they appear at first.

Prevention is always the best treatment for both mental and physical illness. A sensible, balanced approach to the needs of both mind and body are essential. At the same time, the re-thinking of basic aims and priorities and the general approach to life is basic for many people. Both the mental and physical aspects of man are inseparable, and when equal attention is paid to both, it is possible to move towards, and eventually attain a higher level of health and well-being.

SOME TYPICAL CASES

There was a patient aged thirty-seven with a history of chronic low back pain off and on for twenty years. He had received various treatments over the years including manipulation. When I saw him his back was completely seized up and rigid, so that he could barely walk or leave his bed, having rested in bed for the previous ten days without relief. The pain had come on acutely in the car, when bending over at an awkward angle to adjust one of the seats. The pain was worse for rest, particularly for sitting, and definitely helped by heat and warmth. There was tenderness in the right sacroiliac region, and a lot of spasm of the deep muscles supporting the spine on each side of the vertebral column. He was very restless and agitated mentally and physically getting in and out of bed. He was given *Rhus Tox. 10M*, and this was to be followed by *Rhus Tox.* in a low potency four times daily. This led to an improvement, so that the next day he was able to turn over in bed more easily and, two days later, he was definitely better and he could sit and move more easily. On the sixth day he was 70 per cent better and could sit in a chair for periods. There was still a lot of tension in the back, but less pain. A week later he reported being constipated and being rather irritable at home. The improvement had ceased although there was no relapse. *Rhus Tox. 10M* was again followed by *Nux Vomica 6* three times daily. This was followed by further improvement, and a complete return to work and full activity.

*   *   *

There was a married woman aged thirty-six, with chronic sinusitus of four years' duration. The discharge was constant, the nose never stopped pouring a mucous discharge which varied from creamy-yellow to clear. Her nose was very sore, red, running constantly and it bled quite often. The skin around the whole nostril area was red, tender and excoriated. Apart from the severe sinusitis her general health was good. Because of the variable nature of the discharge, her general lack of thirst, easy-going nature, the fairly severe congestion generally, with varicose veins, a tendency to 'flu and retention, and her preference for cool open air rather than the sun, she was prescribed a 10M of *Pulsatilla*.

The result was not encouraging and, because of the insomnia due to catarrh and waking about 4.00 am, *Kali. Bich. 10M* was given. Again she did not respond — the flow became clear mucous and non-stop, the nose bleeding from continual blowing. *Allium Cepa* was prescribed with a slight improvement, but not a clear-cut satisfactory response. *Sulphur* was then given because of her red face and rather untidy appearance, and lack of response to the remedies. After *Sulphur*, a week later she looked better for the first time, the excoriation was less around the nostrils, the face less reddened. *Kali. Bich.* was again prescribed, but this time in low potency, and there was a further improvement. The whole condition slowly cleared up using the same remedy over a period of four weeks.

*   *   *

A woman of forty came with a long history of digestive problems — burning pains in the stomach, aching and soreness, the upper abdomen tender. The stomach felt fine and she had lost two-and-a-half stones in four weeks. She was unable to eat in the mornings at all except for sips of water, and at other meal times she could only take small meals — the food lay heavily on her stomach like lead or glass. The stomach was blown-out and distended and there was a lot of belching of wind. There were also many rectal problems of anal fissure, general discomfort and burning pains. She was given *Thuja* initially, because of the bizarre nature of the stomach complaints, but without a satisfactory response, and this was followed by *Sepia* because of the general nervous depression and irritability and the bearing-down quality to the pains. *Lachesis* followed the *Sepia* — there was a great intolerance of tight clothing. Finally *Sulphur* and *Ornithogalum* were prescribed to complete the recovery.

*   *   *

There was a patient in her late thirties with a history of constipation as far back as she could remember. She sometimes went up to five days without a bowel movement and always had to strain, the stool being hard, dry, lumpy like pebbles and painful. She was always tired, and passed a lot of flatus, the abdomen being very distended. Varicose veins on both legs, and piles, were problems, associated with the straining and chronic constipation. On abdominal examination the colon could be easily felt loaded with hard faeces. Her hair was thinning, she was very fond of sweet foods, rarely sweated and her skin was dry and cool. Her make-up was anxious and generally quite good tempered. *Lycopodium* was prescribed with some improvement, and this was followed by *Bryonia 6* twice daily with a marked easing of symptoms. She was advised to increase the amount of roughage in her diet and to exercise more regularly as additional measures to prevent recurrence.

*   *   *

A woman of twenty-eight came with glandular fever having been diagnosed three weeks earlier. She was tired, had a headache, felt sick, and there were enlarged slightly tender glands behind both ears, and in the upper neck region and groin. For the previous month she had experienced a dull heavy pain in the lower abdomen, was tired and breathless climbing stairs; both legs ached and were tired. She was given *Baryta Carb. 10M* with a marked improvement, remaining well and symptom-free until seen about a year later with tiredness and variable depression after a prolonged period of post-graduate studies. These symptoms cleared quickly also, with *Pulsatilla*, and she has remained well and symptom-free since then.

*   *   *

A patient aged forty-three had had a history of high blood pressure for many years, worse for the stress and strain of her demanding business, and only improved for a complete rest away at a health centre. She tended to eat compulsively and was putting on weight. She was troubled by hot flushes, and her periods were irregular. The ankles were slightly puffy. All emotions were bottled up, so that she remained good tempered on the outside, but was irritable and resentful inside, although this was never shown. Because of the intolerance of heat, intolerance of all fats, and apparently placid nature, she was given *Pulsatilla 10M* which led to an immediate general improvement in the hot flushes, and a general feeling of being more relaxed. Although she was placid externally, she rarely cried, the lower lids were slightly puffy, and she enjoyed being alone, although she rarely had the opportunity. *Natrum Mur.* was then prescribed in high potency, with a further reduction in the pressure reading and a lessening of headaches. Because of the puffy ankles and the general fatigue and tendency to retain fluids, *Crataegus* was given to support the cardio-vascular system. As the blood pressure became stabilized she was kept on *Crataegus* and *Natrum Mur. 6* for a period of several months in order to control the obvious stress factors which were affecting her and to continue to support and strengthen the efficiency of the cardiac muscles and their conducting system.

*   *   *

There was a woman aged twenty-five with a three-year history of rheumatism in her left thumb, index finger, and both knees. The condition began about eight months before her last baby, completely cleared during pregnancy, and recurred soon afterwards. Since then there was burning pain and swelling. Also, after a car crash five years previously, she had developed periodic pains in the ribs of her right side, always worse with damp weather. The condition had been diagnosed as arthritis. Acupuncture had been tried without improvement. The symptoms were generally more severe at night, worse for the heat of the bed, and better for cool applications and elevating the knee. She liked hot sunny weather, iced water, always felt better in the cold and damp, was fearful of thunder, and took a lot of salt in her food. Her make-up was very bright, quick and lively, although she needed a lot of reassurance. *Phosphorus 10M* was prescribed with a moderate improvement, followed by *Rhus Tox*. There was a marked lessening of the symptoms. She came back a few weeks later with a similar pain in the right shoulder which was treated with *Sanguinaria 10M*. Since then she has been symptom-free.

*   *   *

A woman aged thirty-seven came with complaints of headaches over the right temple region which had persisted every day for two years. The pain was worse just before her periods began, and often spread into the right shoulder, right side of the neck and into the base of the skull. She was never free from pain, although the mornings were probably the best time of the day for her. Otherwise she was well, and had been fully investigated at a London hospital without any abnormalities being found. She described herself as a worrier, fussy and irritable, outgoing and liking people. Her taste was for sweet foods but she also took a lot of salt in her food. Her skin was very dry. At times the headache was followed by nausea and vomiting, particularly if there was any excitement or noise. She was given *Lycopodium 10M* with a temporary improvement, followed by a relapse. *Silicea* was then given a month later, after which the headaches were further improved. The final remedy she needed was *Natrum Mur.* in 10M — high potency — which completely cleared up the condition, and she has remained completely symptom-free of all the severe headaches since that time, and only in times of stress does she experience tension and tightening in the area previously affected, but there is no severe pain.

*   *   *

A man of thirty-three came with severe depression, tension, and insomnia. He could not get off to sleep, and when he did the sleep was shallow. He usually felt low, tired and exhausted between 5.00 and 6.00 in the afternoon. Headaches were common, mainly situated in the right temple region. He said that he was very lazy and lethargic, hypochondriacal and that he had been adopted when a few weeks old. He was very nervous, temperamental, too clinging and dependent with people, sensitive and always depressed, but usually beneath the surface. He liked sweet and rich foods, often getting attacks of diarrhoea and flatulence. He was chilly, preferred warm weather, rarely perspired and had a dry skin. He was often quite thirsty. *Lycopodium 10M* was given with an immediate response; the depression and tension becoming much less, he had levelled out, and was sleeping earlier, for longer periods and much more relaxed. The *Lycopodium* was not repeated as the patient continued to improve on the single dosage, and after four weeks was completely well and discharged from any further treatment.

*   *   *

A woman aged thirty-four came complaining of severe chest pain, worse on walking, like a tight band around the chest. As soon as she made any effort to hurry, the pain took her breath away, and made her stop all activity. She had always been healthy and active, careful with her eating habits and watched her weight. About eighteen months previously she had begun to diet and had lost one-and-a-half stones in weight over a period of about six months. However, the dieting began to get out of control and she became too thin and slowly more exhausted, anxious and tired. She could not put on weight again, as hard as she tried. That summer she went with her family to Europe and stayed in a hotel by the seaside. The heat was very intense, even in the shade — where she spent most of the holiday. It was after this period of very hot weather that she developed angina pectoris, after the severe dietary weight loss. She was given *Arnica 10M* initially, followed by *Cactus* and *Lactrodectus* in high potency, and slowly improved over a period of a year. The patient is now free from all pain and able to walk normally.

*   *   *

A woman aged thirty-four came with a history of depression since the birth of a second child two-and-a-half years previously. The depression came on soon after the birth, and made her feel suicidal and indifferent to everything and everybody. She had lost interest in sexuality, and she felt despair and hopelessness, and cried a lot. This had slowly subsided so that eventually she had gone back to work, but she had never really fully recovered, and when I saw her she was severely depressed and getting worse. Everything was an effort and she was worried because she was shouting at the children more and more. Her general health was fairly good, but she had vague joint pains in both hips, fingers and toes, and left jaw. There was also a history of painful periods over the past year, severe pains on the first days with shooting rectal pains and headaches. She was prescribed *Aurum 10M* in view of the severity of her depression, and this resulted in an improvement. Two weeks later she was less depressed, laughing again, and sleep was more refreshing. A month later she was feeling much better and reported that her sexual life was back to normal, and that the joint pains had improved. No further remedy was required, and there had been no recurrence of the depression when seen two years later.

Amenorrhoea (Absence of Menstruation)

Definition　　Absence of the normal period when the cycle has been established normally.

Causes　　Fatigue, shock, travel, debility, exposure to cold or wet prior to onset.

Symptoms　　Failure to menstruate as regularly as usual.

Treatment　　*Pulsatilla; Natrum Mur.; Aconite; Bryonia 30; Belladonna; Sepia; Calc. Carb.; Ferrum Met.; Ignatia; Sulphur.*

Pulsatilla　　Periods always very irregular and variable.

Natrum Mur.　　The periods are scanty, delayed or absent. There is dislike of the seaside and tendency to be solitary, rather timid, nervous, and always tired.

Aconite　　Due to cold.

Bryonia 30　　From chill or fright.

Belladonna　　Colicky, lower abdominal pain, exhaustion and loss of appetite are commonly present. The mood is nearly always one of agitation.

Sepia　　Agonizing pain, depression, wants to be alone.

Calc. Carb.　　Due to anaemia.

Ferrum Met.　　Associated with anaemia, and diarrhoea.

Ignatia　　Due to grief.

Sulphur　　Periods irregular in general.

Anaemia

Definition   A reduced level of haemoglobin in the blood.

Causes   Haemorrhage, menstrual loss, duodenal ulcer, piles, dietary, vitamin deficiency, B12 deficiency in pernicious anaemia.

Symptoms   Pallor, weakness, fainting, lack of drive and initiative.

Treatment   *Ferrum Met.; Arsenicum; Calcarea; Phosphorus; Natrum Mur.; China; Pulsatilla.*

Ferrum Met.   A basic fundamental remedy, with a flushed face and then extreme pallor.

Arsenicum   Useful when there is a combination of great weakness and anxiety and restlessness. Helpful in pernicious anaemia.

Calcarea   Useful in the chalky pallor of the *Calcarea* make up as also *Calc. Phos.* when the patient is less obese.

Phosphorus   Indicated for the tall pale, sensitive and weak person. With little resistance, often short of breath, underweight, with a tendency to be overactive, and rarely to ever rest adequately or to build-up essential energy and body reserves.

Natrum Mur.   Useful when there is loss of weight, breathlessness, depression, palpitations and a good appetite. In a solitary person worse for consolation.

China   When due to loss of fluids as in haemorrhage, excessive menstrual loss.

Pulsatilla   This is very helpful when there is pallor, chilliness and yet intolerance of heat, better in the open air, and absence of thirst.

Anxiety

Definition	The emotional state of anxiety and tension.
Causes	Any emotional trauma or happening in a sensitive temperament; familial; hereditary.
Symptoms	Worry, failure to relax, fear, insomnia, tension, lack of confidence.
Treatment	*Natrum Mur.; Phosphorus; Calcarea; Arsenicum; Pulsatilla.*
Natrum Mur.	This is usually the remedy of choice unless there are contra-indications, or another remedy is more strongly indicated.
Phosphorus	Patient has a need for reassurance and never takes his eye off yours in order to feel secure. They lack confidence but are usually less withdrawn than *Pulsatilla*.
Calcarea	Has a lot of restless anxiety in the plump, pale, weak, sweaty *Calcarea* make-up.
Arsenicum	Is useful in the excessively chilly, restless, fastidious make-up. They are always exhausted.
Pulsatilla	Shy, anxious, emotional, intolerance of heat, crying easily, above all very changeable in symptoms.

Backache (Low)

Definition   Pain in the lumbar sacro-iliac region.

Causes   Local arthritic changes, spinal displacement, rheumatism due to cold or humidity.

Symptoms   Pain, stiffness, impaired mobility, sciatica.

Treatment   *Natrum Mur.; Sepia; Ruta; Rhus Tox.; Calc. Fluor.; Nux Vomica; Arnica.*

Natrum Mur.   Severe chronic backache, especially in a person who takes a lot of salt. The pain is always better for firm pressure.

Sepia   Has chronic dragging down low back ache, worse when sitting and better for a cushion pressing into the area. Constipation, irritability and sallow skin are characteristic.

Ruta   An excellent remedy for low lumbar pain, worse for sitting and lying down. Better for warmth. Rain is often enjoyed provided that they are warm and not chilled.

Rhus Tox.   The condition is usually brought on by exposure to cold, and always better for heat and motion, worse when commencing movement having been immobile. Usually it is better for a firm support or pressure, and bending backwards.

Calc. Fluor.   There is a burning pain, better for continued movement, but worse after rest. The *Calcarea* make-up is characteristic.

Nux Vomica   Low back pain, usually worse at night in bed, so that the person has to sit up in order to turn over. The pain is dull and severe, at times darting in character. There is often a morning aggravation. Constipation and irritability are common.

Arnica   When backache follows trauma.

Bronchitis

Definition   Infection of the bronchial lining mucosa.

Causes   Acute infection, often in recurrent form, where there is a
                    disposition (may follow pneumonia, flu).

Symptoms   Cough, fever, there may be mild shortness of breath, and
                    mild wheezing, but the main symptom is cough.

Treatment   *Aconite; Bryonia; Belladonna; Phosphorus; Ant. Tart.;
                    Kali. Bich.*

Aconite   The earliest remedy to be given only within the first
                    twenty-four hours. There is a short dry cough, a
                    temperature and an irritation in the throat and chest and
                    trachea. The cause is usually due to exposure to cold.
                    There is a chilly restlessness, anxiety and a full bounding
                    pulse, with general weakness.

Bryonia   There is a painful, violent, dry, sticking cough, with
                    headache, and pains in the chest wall, worse for cough-
                    ing and better for supporting the area with both hands.
                    The expectoration is yellow often blood-streaked. The
                    cough is worse after meals.

Belladonna   The patient has a high temperature, dry cough,
                    pounding, pulsating headache, a flushed face, with a dry
                    hot skin. The cough is worse at night and for lying down.

Phosphorus   This is a useful remedy for tall and pale people with little
                    natural resistance, bright-eyed and very anxious,
                    needing constant reassurance. Breathing is often tight
                    with wheezing, a dry tickling cough and sore chest,
                    worse for talking and fresh air.

Ant. Tart.   When there is an accumulation of considerable, loose,
                    rattling, moist mucus in the chest. Useful in children
                    and old age — with a rattling wheezy breathing and a
                    loose cough, but little phlegm is expectorated. There
                    may be vomiting and breathing is laboured. Exhaustion
                    is marked.

Kali. Bich.   Less acute in form. The phlegm is tough, thick and stringy, and cannot easily be expectorated. There is a tightness of the chest and a troublesome cough. Worse at 4.00 to 5.00 am.

Cancer Phobia

Definition   Anxiety, tense phobic state, dominated by the obsessional fear of cancer.

Causes   Depression, obsessional and sometimes delusional make-up.

Symptoms   Preoccupation, hypochondriasis, self-absorbed.

Treatment   *Lycopodium; Nux Vomica; Arsenicum; Pulsatilla.*

Lycopodium   This is one of the most useful remedies for hypochondriasis (preoccupation with the body symptoms) where the slightest ache or pain is translated into the most dramatic illness.

Nux Vomica   This is useful when there is irritability, tension due to excessive over-working and business worries with added abuse of alcohol or stimulants.

Arsenicum   Helpful when the preoccupation is obsessional and associated with severe weakness, collapse and debility.

Pulsatilla   Useful in timid, weepy, anxious, insecure and frightened young women.

Carbuncles

Definition   A large suppurative swelling up to six inches diameter, usually on back, buttocks, or neck, reddish-blue overlying skin.

Causes   Usually occurs in a debilitated state, cause often unknown.

Symptoms   Pain, fever, swelling, depression, irritability, general malaise. May discharge at several points, slow to clear.

Treatment   *Anthracinum; Silicea; Apis; Lachesis; Borax* compress; *Tarentula; Arsenicum; Belladonna.*

Anthracinum   Blueness, blistering and angry appearance, with black centre.

Silicea   Intense pain, burning, foetid pus and green of underlying tissue.

Apis   Indicated where there is very considerable swelling, tension and redness to surrounding tissues.

Lachesis   When blueness predominates.

Borax compress   Useful in difficult infected chronic cases. Slow to heal. Patient often has a temperature.

Tarentula   When the pain is very severe.

Arsenicum   Large painful malignant carbuncles, with prostration.

Belladonna   Shiny red, stabbing pains before pus forms.

Catarrh

Definition	Catarrhal inflammation of the mucous lining layer of the nose and sinuses.
Causes	Usually acute infection, more likely when resistance and vitality is lowered.
Symptoms	Catarrhal discharge, the exudate is white, yellow or green, depending on the degree of infection.
Treatment	*Pulsatilla; Nux Vomica; Arsenicum; Kali. Carb.; Kali. Bich.; Allium Cepa; Mercurius; Kali. Iod.*
Pulsatilla	The catarrh is variable in frequency and intensity, with a discharge which may be clear, yellow or green. Usually worse in the evening and at night. They are chilly but prefer a cool room with the windows open for fresh air.
Nux Vomica	Useful in the early stages of a cold with associated nasal catarrh, often dry. Constipation, backache and irritability tend to be associated.
Arsenicum	There is a copious burning excoriating clear watery discharge, chilliness, craving for heat, great prostration, agitation, sneezing and watering eyes are associated.
Kali. Carb.	The catarrh is thick and yellow, worse in the morning and evening, and worse for a dry hot atmosphere. Sore throat, sneezing and swelling of the upper lids is characteristic.
Kali. Bich.	The discharge is thick yellow and infected, with a sore throat, hoarseness and tough stringy mucus. Often there is a cough associated and worse between 4.00 and 5.00 am.
Allium Cepa	There is a very profuse watery discharge, sneezing and burning excoriation of the nose and lip areas.
Mercurius	The breath is foul, and the throat is infected, the discharge is thick yellow, often with enlarged and tender cervical glands.

Kali. Iod.   There is a thin, burning discharge, hot and acrid, with puffy eyes and a sore throat. The nose is red and irritated.

Chilblains

Definition   Low grade inflammatory condition of the skin, provoked by cold climatic condition, and associated with poor general circulation of the skin.

Causes   Exposure with inadequate protection, warming the chilled parts, poor circulation.

Symptoms   Redness/blueness, itching and slight swelling of parts affected, usually hands and feet, may ulcerate.

Treatment   *Agaricus; Rhus Tox.; Sulphur; Pulsatilla; Carbo Veg.; Nux Vomica; Petroleum; Calc. Carb.; Belladonna;* Locally *Tamus* ointment, or *Calendula.*

Agaricus   Redness, burning, itching, worse when cold.

Rhus Tox.   Inflammed with itching.

Sulphur   Itching, worse from warmth, obstinate cases.

Pulsatilla   Blueish, pricking-burning pain, worse in the evening.

Carbo Veg.   The chilblains itch and burn, particularly from warmth in bed. Helps to improve the circulation generally in the area affected.

Nux Vomica   Tense, irritable, worse for wind and draughts.

Petroleum   When broken and cracked with tendency to ulcerate, itching and burning, chaps and split finger tips.

Calc. Carb.   Feet damp and cold, better for cold.

Belladonna   Bright red, swelling and pulsating.

Tamus ointment   A useful specific remedy, particularly when there is blueness to the affected area.

Calendula   Stimulates healing. May be applied locally as a tincture, or taken internally.

Common Cold

Definition   An acute upper respiratory tract infection, catarrhal in type.

Causes   An acute viral infection.

Symptoms   Sneezing, headache, fever, sore throat, swollen eyes and throat with usually a profuse nasal discharge, either clear or thick and purulent.

Treatment   *Aconite; Bryonia; Gelsemium; Arsenicum; Pulsatilla; Nux Vomica; Mercurius; Allium Cepa.*

Aconite   Early stages especially after exposure to cold, feverish, sneezing, thirsty, burning and rawness of palate, worse in stuffy atmosphere.

Bryonia   Hard, dry, shaking cough, worse in the daytime, often with stitch-like pain in the side and chest, worse from cold, thirsty for large quantities of cold water. Holds chest and head when coughing.

Gelsemium   For the mild, acute cold, with a marked sense of shivering and chilliness. There is a watery discharge, the throat hot and dry.

Arsenicum   Abundant thin, hot, acid excoriating mucus, burning discharges and sensation, lassitude and prostration.

Pulsatilla   Impaired taste and smell, thick yellow discharge (yellow-green) worse in evening or warm room, symptoms variable, better out-of-doors.

Nux Vomica   One of the best remedies, nose feels tight, headache, constipation.

Mercurius   Sweating from a febrile exhausting cold with severe infection of the throat. A foul greenish-yellow mucus is coughed up.

Allium Cepa   Profuse watery discharge, sneezing, nose and lips sore and raw, worse in a warm room, better for fresh air.

Concussion

Definition　　Loss of consciousness, due to trauma to the head, the period and depth of the loss of consciousness varying with the degree of trauma.

Causes　　Trauma.

Symptoms　　Loss of consciousness, shock, confusion, pallor, cold extremities.

Treatment　　*Arnica; Hypericum; Ruta* tincture locally; *Aconite; Opium; Veratum Alb.; Belladonna; Natrum Sulph.*

Arnica　　This is always the first treatment to give, and the most basic and important.

Hypericum　　The head feels heavy and painful and is extremely sensitive to the least touch or movement. Confusion is marked.

Ruta　　Tincture locally applied.

Aconite　　A useful remedy following *Arnica* if there is a flushed face (red) and bounding pulse with restlessness and a raised temperature.

Opium　　Heavy breathing, constipation, after the concussion. Rattling in the throat.

Veratum Alb.　　Collapse, coldness, sweating, particularly on the forehead. Shocked. Face cold, pale, sweating, weak pulse.

Belladonna　　Headache, flushed face, bounding pulse, irritable, restless.

Natrum Sulph.　　Pain is severe and tearing. Dizziness and vomiting is often a feature.

Constipation

Definition   Irregular and erratic bowel action, with the failure to establish a normal daily rhythm of evacuation.

Causes   Faulty bowel training, dietary, lack of exercise, convalescence, change of environment, fever, illness, megacolon.

Treatment   *Collinsonia; Nux Vomica; Bryonia; Alumina; Natrum Mur.; Opium; Plumbum.*

Collinsonia   Useful in obstinate cases. The stools are hard and considerable straining is needed. Often there is an associated weakness and feeling of faintness. Rheumatism and piles are often present.

Nux Vomica   Useful when there is a long history of loss of bowel habit, due to laxatives and inattention to regular bowel habits, lack of exercise. There is a chronic constant ineffective irregular urging, which is incomplete and unsatisfactory.

Bryonia   The stool is hard and dry and passed with an absence of normal urging. Stools passed with great difficulty.

Alumina   There is a dryness of the stool with complete and total lack of intestinal activity.

Natrum Mur.   There is a crumbly hard stool, difficult to expel and often associated with bleeding and ineffectual urging.

Opium   There is an absolute and complete inaction of the intestines with no desire or urge, and the faeces become impacted and are hard, dry and black.

Plumbum   There is constipation with colic and urging to go to stool, only passing with difficulty, hard, black, round, dry balls with a spasm as if drawn upwards.

Cramps (Nocturnal)

Definition   Limb cramps, often in the legs, usually at night.

Causes   Often unknown, circulatory, salt depletion, from excessive sweating.

Treatment   *Nux Vomica; Cuprum Met.; Acetic Acid; Gelsemium; Chamomilla; Iris Vers.; Verat. Alb.*

Nux Vomica   When associated with headache, loss of appetite, nausea, constipation.

Cuprum Met.   Usually in the feet and legs.

Acetic Acid   Stomach pains, especially in the pale, anaemic person, with marked debility.

Gelsemium   Burning pains of the arms and legs. Writer's cramp. Irritability is nearly always a feature. Usually the symptoms are better for movement of the affected part.

Chamomilla   When associated and located in thighs and legs.

Iris Vers.   When associated with diarrhoea.

Verat. Alb.   Particularly, cramps of the calf muscles, better for local massage, but often worsens by walking about.

HEALING · ARTS · PRESS

If you wish to receive a copy of the latest INNER TRADITIONS INTERNATIONAL catalog and to be placed on our mailing list, please send us this card.

Name _____   Date _____

Address _____

_____

City _____   State _____ Zip _____

(Please Print)

HAP

INNER TRADITIONS INTERNATIONAL, INC.

One Park Street

Rochester, VT 05767

Depression

Definition	A depressive state of mind.
Causes	Loss, age, shock, separation, familial, constitutional.
Symptoms	Depression, fatigue, insomnia, weakness, no drive, lack of interest, despair, various physical symptoms, and aches and pains.
Treatment	*Aurum; Sepia; Natrum Mur.*
Aurum	This is the most useful remedy when there is depression and a suicidal tendency. They cannot be coaxed out of their depression.
Sepia	They are depressed and irritable, dragged down by the cares and responsibilities of the day.
Natrum Mur.	Usually less severely depressed than *Aurum* and more emotional, often hysterical. Tendency to be solitary. They may sometimes make a suicidal gesture but it is more a gesture than a determined attempt, although tragedies may occur.

Dysmenorrhoea (Painful Menstruation)

Definition	Discomfort and pain during the cycle, either before or during the flow.
Causes	Constitutional, familial, fibroids.
Symptoms	Cramping pains, discomfort, nausea, headache, flow may be scanty with clots, low back or abdominal pain.
Treatment	*Pulsatilla; Chamomilla; Mag. Phos.; Gelsemium; Sulphur; Belladonna; Viburnum Op.; Cimicifuga.*
Pulsatilla	Cutting and tearing pains, lower abdomen and back, loss of appetite, chill, diarrhoea during period, scanty or profuse loss, clots, gentle disposition.
Chamomilla	Blood 'dirty' with clots, labour-like pains, frequency, irritable.
Mag. Phos.	Spasm-like pain of a colicy nature.
Gelsemium	There are spasms of sharp pains felt in the lower abdomen and back, usually better for the application of local heat.
Sulphur	Periods irregular and the pain has a burning character to it.
Belladonna	Pain one day before the flow, intestines feel forced through the vagina, defaecation painful, cutting pains, face red and throbbing.
Viburnum Op.	Sudden onset of pain, spreading over the whole uterus. Spasmodic.
Cimicifuga	Headache — pre-menses. Labour-type pain in lower abdomen, clots.

Fainting

Definition   Partial loss of consciousness and muscular power, of short duration.

Causes   Emotional, weakness, convalescent, fatigue, anaemia.

Symptoms   Pallor, nausea, dizziness, sweating, temporary loss of consciousness.

Treatment   *Aconite; Opium; Ammoniacum; Carboneum; Veratrum Viride; Arsenicum; Natrum Mur.; Digitalis; China; Camphor; Ammonium Carbonate.*

Aconite   Especially when due to fear or emotional excitement.

Opium   Drowsy and fainting from fear.

Ammoniacum   Fainting in cold weather. Nausea. The throat is dry and full. Irritability is a marked feature.

Carboneum   Where there is a tendency to spasm in any part of the body. During or following the fainting pallor and coldness is marked.

Veratum Viride   The body is covered with an icy cold sweat and is weak and prostrated.

Arsenicum   Restless, chilly, sweating.

Natrum Mur.   When there is a predominantly emotional or hysterical cause.

Digitalis   When associated with heart disease.

China   When due to weakness and debility, often after a long illness.

Camphor   The tincture, may be given as 'smelling salts' to revive.

*Ammonium
   Carbonate*   The patient lies listless and immobile.

Fatigue

Definition   Tiredness, lassitude, and absence of energy.

Causes   Many, but usually failure to take regular breaks, anaemia, suppression, almost any physical condition, convalescence.

Symptoms   Lack of energy and reserve.

Treatment   *China; Arnica; Arsenicum; Carbo Veg.; Nux Vomica; Phosphoric Acid.*

China   An excellent remedy for the fatigue following a prolonged exhaustive illness, or the psychological weakness after a prolonged period of disturbance whilst nursing an invalid relative.

Arnica   When the fatigue is muscular in origin and characterized by aches and pains and exhaustion.

Arsenicum   Nothing is more exhausted, cold and chilly than *Arsenicum*, and excellent for the fatigue following an attack of flu or when generally run down. There is an associated restlessness and inability to relax which is characteristic.

Carbo Veg.   For extreme exhaustion and cold extremities, poor circulation and cold clammy sweating.

Nux Vomica   When there is spasm, pain and weariness with a feeling as if the joints are bruised. There is often a trembling sensation and weakness of the legs.

Phosphoric Acid   A tonic when there is general weakness and fatigue, profuse cold clammy sweats, weakness on exertion. Often the hair is weak and thinning. The exhaustion may be due to a prolonged or chronic illness, sometimes too rapid growth in an adolescent, or flooding at the menopause.

Flatulence

Definition   Sensation of being bloated and distended after meals.

Causes   Indigestion, peptic ulcer, dietary.

Symptoms   Fullness pain and discomfort after meals.

Treatment   *Carbo Veg.; Lycopodium; Nux Vomica; Argent. Nit.; China; Chamomilla.*

Carbo Veg.   Flatulence, pain and wind in the upper abdominal region.

Lycopodium   Flatulence in the lower abdomen.

Nux Vomica   Flatulence associated with constipation, constricting pain and belching which is bitter tasting.

Argent. Nit.   A useful remedy for abdominal pain and flatulence, always intolerant of heat.

China   Especially involving the upper abdominal area. Weakness is a feature. The area is very tender to touch, but better for firm pressure and warmth.

Chamomilla   Flatulence of infants, better after bringing up wind and associated with irritability.

Floaters

Definition   Small semi-transparent, sometimes bright, particles that float in the field of vision, often on change of position, usually short-lasting.

Causes   Unknown.

Symptoms   The discomfort of the floaters, in the field of vision.

Treatment   *China; Phosphoric Acid.*

China   Useful when associated with general weakness and fatigue.

Phosphoric Acid   Follows well after *China*.

Flooding

Definition   There is a heavy loss, often unexpected, during the menstrual flow, may be associated with clots.

Causes   Menopause, fibroids, endometriosis, tumour.

Symptoms   Heavy loss, may be prolonged for the whole of the five days or more.

Treatment   *Borax; Mag. Carb.; Arsenicum; Pulsatilla; Sabina; Lachesis; Crocus Sat.; Ustilago* tincture.

Borax   The periods are too profuse and too frequent, there is lower abdominal cramping pain.

Mag. Carb.   There is a profuse discharge, worse at night.

Arsenicum   Weakness and excessive flooding.

Pulsatilla   When the flooding is associated with pain in the lower abdomen and back. The symptoms are always variable and changing.

Sabina   Especially indicated in obese women with pain in the ovaries and the passage of bright red blood.

Crocus Sat.   The flooding is painless, offensive, often clots are passed and it is dark, worsened by any movement.

Ustilago   A very useful remedy for severe cases with black clots often associated with thinning of the hair. Always worse for heat. May be taken as the tincture if severe.

Lachesis   Especially when there is severe cramp pains and hot flushes. Anger and irritability is marked.

Flu

Definition	Acute infection by the influenza virus.
Causes	Usually epidemic influenza.
Symptoms	Prostration, fever, catarrhal symptoms, muscular pains.
Treatment	*Aconite; Gelsemium; Arsenicum; Nux Vomica; Bryonia; Influenzinium.* General treatment: Bed rest and fluids only until the temperature is normal.
Aconite	In early stages with fever, rigors and chill, particularly in children.
Gelsemium	For early cases with temperature, fatigue, weakness and general aching and soreness in the whole of the body, particularly in the back area. The patient is chilly, has a cough, the face is flushed, the eyes water, and sneezing is frequent.
Arsenicum	One of the best remedies when there is exhaustion, weakness and prostration, chilliness and restlessness with anxiety. Burning pains are characteristic and there is a profuse acid burning nasal discharge, with sneezing, thirst and conjunctivitis. Diarrhoea is commonly associated.
Nux Vomica	One of the best early remedies for acute flu. The patient is constipated, irritable, and has general body aches and pains, particularly in the back region.
Bryonia	There is a dry cough, fever, generalized body pain, particularly in the chest wall. Dryness is a feature of the lips and tongue. The patient lies prostrate and motionless, as there is aggravation from the least jar or movement.
Influenzinium	The nosode may be indicated in certain severe refractory cases.

Frigidity

Definition   Inability to respond and participate in normal sexual intercourse.

Causes   Many, but usually psychological; immaturity; trauma; constitutional.

Symptoms   Tension, pain, anxiety, absence of normal responses and pleasure.

Treatment   *Natrum Mur.; Pulsatilla; Argent. Nit.; Silicea; Belladonna; Ignatia.*

Natrum Mur.   When the anxiety, fear and inability to relax is marked. Helpful when the problem is acute and recent, or associated with a psychological trauma.

Pulsatilla   For the timid, fair-haired, tearful immature girl. Passive and variable in all things. Never the same from one day to the next. There is also great intolerance of heat.

Argent. Nit.   For the more phobic personality. Worse for heat, but in general more mature and assertive than the *Pulsatilla* make-up.

Silicea   Of value in more long-standing cases.

Belladonna   When there is marked pain and spasm.

Ignatia   Helpful when the main factors are based on fear, immaturity and anxiety.

Gall-Stone Colic

Definition   Severe spasms of colic pain in the gall-bladder area.

Causes   Gall-stones.

Symptoms   Pain, sweating, collapse, doubling-up pain.

Treatment   *Mag. Carb.; Berberis* tincture; *Dioscorea; Veratrum Album; Chelidonium.*

Mag. Carb.   One of the best remedies for griping doubling-up pain.

Berberis tincture Given every five to ten minutes relaxes the spasms.

Dioscoria   For severe umbilical pain, relieved by stretching the body backwards. The pains often radiate to the chest and back.

Veratrum Album   For pains which double-up, or require walking around for relief. There is a cold sweat and considerable flatulence and distension with constipation.

Chelidonium   Often a useful remedy in gall-bladder problems.

Glandular Fever

Definition	An acute infection, of children and adults, with marked glandular involvement.
Causes	Contact.
Symptoms	Intermittent fever, general malaise and weakness, enlarged spleen. General glandular involvement.
Treatment	*Belladonna; Calcarea; Phytolacca; Baryta Carb.* The specific Nosode.
Belladonna	When there is high fever and glandular involvement.
Calcarea	When growth is retarded, and there is profuse sweating.
Phytolacca	Headaches are common, mainly of the forehead, and there is chronic nasal catarrh with sudden generalized pains which come and go. Lymph glands are enlarged, sore and burning.
Baryta Carb.	Of value for the glandular symptoms.
The Nosode	Indicated in acute cases and for prevention.

Glaucoma

Definition	Increased pressure in the intraocular eyeball.
Causes	Hypertension, senility, degeneration.
Symptoms	Pain, visual impairment.
Treatment	*Aconite; Opium; Spigelia; Gelsemium; Bryonia; Phosphorus;* Glaucoma should only be treated by a physician and not by the family.
Aconite	In the acute form of glaucoma *Aconite* is indicated.
Opium	The eyeballs seem expanded and large and under pressure. Vision is misty and reduced, the pupils fixed.
Spigelia	The eyeball feels too large and pulled back into the head. Of great value in the sharp, shooting, sticking pains of glaucoma — particularly worse for movement and at night. Palpitations are often associated.
Gelsemium	One of the most useful remedies in glaucoma. Double vision is frequent, the vision misty and diminished. The eyes feel bruised and under pressure.
Bryonia	The intraocular tension is raised and there is intense soreness, watering and photophobia.
Phosphorus	Is useful to diminish the pain and limit degeneration changes.
Belladonna	Indicated when the onset is violent and acute with inflammation, dryness and photophobia.

ACUTE ILLNESSES OF ADULT COUPLES 149

Goitre

Definition	Swelling of the thyroid gland.
Causes	Either over-activity or under-activity of the thyroid gland.
Symptoms	Loss of weight, fatigue, palpitations, protrusion of eyeballs — (over-activity). Lassitude, dry skin, falling hair, tendency to obesity — (under-activity).
Treatment	*Thyroidinum; Natrum Mur.; Iodium; Spongia; Calc. Iod.; Calc. Carb.* The treatment should be directed by a physician, and not attempted initially by the patient or the family.
Thyroidinum	Useful when there is an exopthalmic toxic goitre with loss of weight, headache, sweating, tremor, rapid pulse, and agitation.
Natrum Mur.	One of the best remedies for exophthalmic goitre and an over-active thyroid gland, with the typical palpitations and weight loss.
Iodium	Useful in simple and toxic goitres, with exophthalmus, where there is a rapid pulse, agitation and weight loss.
Spongia	Useful in simple non-toxic goitres due to iodine deficiency — as in 'Derbyshire neck'.
Calc. Iod.	Useful in simple non-toxic goitre problems in children and adults.
Calc. Carb.	Useful in simple non-toxic goitre problems in children and adults.

Gout

Definition	A febrile disease, associated with periodic paroxysms of inflammation and swelling of the joints of the hands and feet with excessive uric acid levels in the blood.
Causes	The accumulation of uric acid in the tissues of the joints affected caused by a prolonged period of dietary indiscretion with alcohol and foods rich in animal fats and of high protein content.
Symptoms	Pain, redness and heat usually in the joint of the great toe.
Treatment	*Belladonna; Colchicum; Arnica; Aconite; Ledum; Urtica Urens; Ammon. Phos.*
Belladonna	The affected joint is red, hot, swollen and unbearably tender, sensitive to the least touch or jolt, or movement. Better for cold compresses and exposure to cool air.
Colchicum	Indicated where there is a swelling usually of the great toe, which is red and very tender to touch often with a tendency to shift about. The pain often shifts from one joint to another. Usually there is associated abdominal fullness and a sense of weakness. Irritability and anger is common. One of the best remedies.
Arnica	Is indicated when the pain is of a bruised sprained type.
Aconite	Useful in very acute painful cases.
Ledum	Pain in ball of great toe, worse from warmth, pain and movement. There is little swelling associated. Cases are very chilly, and there may be gout nodules in other joints.
Urtica Urens	Another very useful remedy, particularly for acute gout. There is an intense burning and itching, with swelling of the affected area.
Ammon. Phos.	For chronic cases with nodules.

Haematemesis

Definition   The vomiting of blood, usually fresh and bright red.

Causes   Swallowing of blood from epistaxis, after dental extraction, peptic ulcer, Aspirin irritation of stomach wall.

Symptoms   The symptoms are of the blood in the vomit.

Treatment   *Arnica.* This condition calls for immediate medical attention and hospitalization. Keep patient warm and quiet in bed until the ambulance arrives.

Arnica   May be given every ten to fifteen minutes to help combat the shock of loss of blood. Use the 6c potency.

Hay Fever

Definition   An acute seasonal catarrhal allergic complaint of the sinus and nasal mucosa.

Causes   Allergy to grass and other pollens.

Symptoms   All the symptoms of an acute cold, with running eyes, sneezing, catarrh and insomnia.

Treatment   *Teucrium;* Mixed Pollen.*; Kali. Carb.; Arsenicum; Sabadilla; Allium Cepa.*

Teucrium   One of the most helpful spring grass remedies.

Mixed Pollen   The potentized Mixed Pollen is very useful in late summer and early autumn hay fever.

Kali. Carb.   Is a very useful remedy with severe hay fever, worse in the morning and evening. Symptoms include a clear or yellow thick discharge, sore throat, sneezing, and watering of the eyes. Swelling of the eyelids is characteristic. Usually they are worse for being inside and are relieved by fresh air.

Arsenicum   There is a thin burning and excoriating watery discharge, with sneezing and catarrh, worse after midnight, and restlessness.

Sabadilla   Useful in hay fever with profuse watery discharge, sneezing and frontal sinus headache.

Allium Cepa   Itching is marked, of the nose and eyes, with a very profuse clear nasal discharge which is acid and excoriating.

Headache

Definition   Pain and discomfort in the head and upper cervical region.

Causes   Multiple and varied, commonly just before a cold, infection, or a sign of fever in acute ear and throat infections.

Symptoms   Dull or throbbing ache, dizziness, sensitivity to light, nausea, loss of appetite, irritability.

Treatment   *Pulsatilla; Ignatia; Arnica; Belladonna; Iris; Glonoine; Gelsemium; Nux Vomica; Aconite; Cocculus; Silica.*

Pulsatilla   Periodic, throbbing, variable, weeping, associated with indigestion of fatty and starchy food. Better for cool applications, open air, and slow walking. Worse for looking up and lying down.

Ignatia   There is a band-like pressure headache across the forehead with dizziness, nausea, often associated with a show of emotion and weeping.

Arnica   Bruised-like headache, mainly of the forehead region, worsened by any movement.

Belladonna   Burning throbbing headache, worse for light and noise, face red, worse for lying-down, jar, stooping, coughing, straining at stool. Eyes too large. Better for wrapping head up warmly.

Iris   Right-sided headaches with vomiting of bile, usually worse in the evening or early morning hours.

Glonoine   Due to exposure to the sun, throbbing, increased urination, terrible bursting throbbing pains. Worse, sun, heat, jar. Better, cool air, lying down, sleep, head held high.

Gelsemium   Giddiness and nausea associated with right-sided headache, often over the eye or temple. The pain is worse for movement, noise and light.

Nux Vomica   Splitting headache, after eating, with giddiness and irritability, constipation often associated, spasmodic and throbbing, splitting in the temple region, nausea and vomiting. Worse after meals and stooping, often worse in the morning on waking, after alcohol, or in the open air. Better with warmth, lying down, covering head.

Aconite Head feels congested, hemicrania, throbbing of temples, eyes, violent sudden headache, band-like, restless anxious, thirsty. Better for rest. Worse for noise and movement.

Cocculus Sick headache, retching, little vomiting.

Silica The headache usually appears in the occipital region, spreading upwards to involve the whole head area. Better for wrapping the whole head warmly. Profuse sweating is a common feature.

Hydrocele

Definition An accumulation of fluid in the sac surrounding the testicle.

Causes Congenital usually.

Symptoms Swelling of the testicle area.

Treatment *Graphites; Pulsatilla; Iodum; Rhododendron; Rhus Tox.; Arnica.*

Graphites Swelling of the testes which may be severe and involve the whole penis. A moist overlying eczema is commonly present.

Pulsatilla Usually affects the left testicle and is painless and slowly increases in size.

Iodum Helpful in some cases. The testicle often aches and is swollen and hard. Symptoms are worsened by heat of any kind.

Rhododendron Useful in acute hydrocele when right sided. Often discomfort before a storm.

Rhus Tox. Useful when worse for cold.

Arnica When caused by injury.

Hypochondriasis

Definition   A psychological preoccupation with illness and body symptoms, either real or imaginary.

Causes   An abnormal preoccupation with health and the body which may be psychological, post illness, or caused by trauma.

Symptoms   Any pain or symptom is translated into a serious illness.

Treatment   *Lycopodium.*

Lycopodium   This is one of the best remedies — usually in an intellectual non-sporting person of sedentary occupation preoccupied with his own body and any symptoms which may develop. Usually cases have problems with both the digestive system and with sleeping which is shallow and intermittent. A dry skin and craving for sweet foods is characteristic.

Impotence

Definition   Failure to achieve an erection which is adequate for normal intercourse and penetration.

Causes   Usually psychological; fatigue, debility; anaemia, diabetes.

Symptoms   Impotence, often after an initial erection, often worsened by consciously trying.

Treatment   *Lycopodium; Arnica; Agnus Castus; Argent. Nit. Conium; Sabal Serrulata.*

Lycopodium   This is a useful remedy in more persistent cases.

Arnica   When there is a temporary impotence not psychological in type, associated with trauma and bruising.

Agnus Castus   Of value in the earliest stages of the problem.

Argent. Nit.   When there is marked anxiety and fear of intercourse.

Conium   A useful adjunct remedy.

Sabal Serrulata When the impotence occurs in the elderly and is associated with debility.

Infertility

Definition   The failure to conceive after repeated attempts.

Causes   Multiple; the problem may be in the male or female, determined by sperm profile. Immaturity, stress, debility.

Symptoms   Pregnancy does not occur.

Treatment   Constitutional remedy; *Conium; Borax; Iodum; Sepia; Aurum; Phosphorus; Natrum Mur.; Silicea.*
The Constitutional remedy is most useful initially.

Conium   Very valuable when associated with painful breasts, scanty weak periods.

Borax   When there is an associated leucorrhoea.

Iodum   A useful adjunct remedy for thin emaciated women unable to put on weight but always hungry and always eating. Quite intolerant of heat.

Sepia   As above where exhaustion, irritability, loss of libidinal interest and apathy are marked. All symptoms are worse in the evening.

Aurum   As above, especially where depression is a feature.

Phosphorus   As above for the slim woman, outgoing and vivacious, who likes people and is popular. The periods are profuse and often late with burning pains. Libidinal interest is often intense.

Natrum Mur.   As above where nervous features are marked. Tearful, wants to be left alone, consolation, basically anxious and insecure.

Silicea   This is another very useful remedy which has given good results.

Insomnia

Definition   Failure to sleep and establish a normal sleep pattern.

Causes   Tension, pain, excitement of anticipation, over-activity, cerebral disease, dietary, coffee, tea and stimulants, depression, restlessness.

Symptoms   Inability to relax and sleep, may wake from sleep.

Treatment   *Coffea; Chamomilla; Nux Vomica; Pulsatilla; Passiflora; Lycopodium: Cocculus.*

Coffea   Useful for insomnia following excessive coffee drinking, particularly when there is tension and agitation, wide-awake with no tendency to sleep.

Chamomilla   The great remedy for children unable to sleep because of pain, excitement or irritability.

Nux Vomica   Sleepy in the evening, the sleep is fitful and not deep, wakes between 2.00 and 3.00 am. Often useful when there is excessive studying, overwork, in excessive coffee and tea drinkers.

Pulsatilla   Unable to fall asleep until after midnight, then wakes again about 3.00 am, often to walk about or have a snack or cold drink. They are always worse in a warm room and sleep with arms above the head.

Passiflora   Useful for restless sleep. Nervous and excitable in the late evening, the mind over-active and over-charged with ideas and worries.

Lycopodium   Useful when there is an overactive mind in the late evening, worrying about the day's happenings, unable to fall asleep until the early hours, and then sleeps soundly.

Cocculus   This is a useful remedy when the person is exhausted, over-tired, may have been nursing or caring for an invalid over a prolonged period. Usually their minds are over-active in bed, and they tend to be irritable and slightly giddy.

Irregular Periods

Definition   The periods are unpredictable and there is not the normal twenty-eight day cycle, but a variation in length and period of flow.

Causes   Fibroids, pre-menopause, stress, convalescence, travelling, infection, menopause, anaemia.

Symptoms   The periods are irregular and unpredictable.

Treatment   *Conium; Pulsatilla; China.*

Conium   The periods are irregular and there is often an associated painful swelling of the breasts.

Pulsatilla   Useful in a variable, irregular menstrual cycle. Usually scanty, delayed, or suppressed, pale watery discharge.

China   The periods are irregular, often too long and profuse with associated dark clots.

Laryngitis

Definition   Infection of the vocal chords, temporary or permanent.

Causes   Infection, emotion, tumour, shock.

Symptoms   Loss of voice, with a hoarseness or husky voice, at times the throat is dry and sore.

Treatment   *Causticum; Arnica; Oxalic Acid; Phosphorus; Aconite; Belladonna; Argent. Nit.; Hepar Sulph.; Carbo Veg.*

Causticum   One of the best remedies with hoarseness and a dry rawness in the throat which is experienced under the sternum and in the chest also. There is an associated hollow irritating cough. Often the voice is totally lost and he can only speak in a whisper.

Arnica   The larynx feels sore and swollen. An irritating cough is frequent. Particularly useful when the cause has been shock or fear.

Oxalic Acid   Severe laryngitis with a painful and raw sensation. Considerable lowering and deepening of the voice.

Phosphorus   There is a characteristic hoarseness worse in the evening and a sore dryness in the larynx with a rough voice, and talking is painful. A dry cough is often present.

Aconite   For acute cases, due usually to exposure to a cold wind or draught. There is often a dry croupy very hot night restlessness, a temperature and anxiety. The patient is chilly, has a dry skin, and the voice is hoarse.

Belladonna   Useful when there is a high temperature a red flushed face dilated pupils sweating and pain in the throat with a dry barking cough.

Argent. Nit.   Indicated in severe phobic or hysterical laryngitis. Often one chord is paralyzed for months for no apparent reason. The symptoms are always aggravated from warmth and better in open-air conditions.

Hepar Sulph.   This is a useful remedy for hoarseness always worse in the morning, caused and worsened by a dry cold wind or draught and better for warmth. The hoarseness of singers or public speakers responds well to it.

Carbo. Veg.   For painless hoarseness, usually caused by exposure to damp cold air, usually worse in evenings, chilly or sweating, with poor circulation.

Leucorrhoea

Definition   Vaginal discharge, white or clear usually.

Causes   Catarrhal inflammation of the vaginal lining mucosa or cervix.

Symptoms   The discharge, with irritation and discomfort.

Treatment   *Calc. Carb.; Alumina; Sepia; Nitric Acid; Kreosote; Borax; Pulsatilla.*

Calc. Carb.   Persistent, milky, yellow discharge, cold damp hands and feet. Helpful in children and girls before puberty. There is often an associated burning pain in the uterus and morning hunger is characteristic.

Alumina   There is a thin irritating, burning white discharge, either before or following a period.

Sepia   There is an offensive yellowish green discharge which is excoriating, worse before the period. There is associated constipation and a sallow face. Of value in infantile leucorrhoea. Cramping uterine pains are common.

Nitric Acid   One of the best remedies when leucorrhoea is associated with chronic ill health and debility, where there is a thick greenish offensive discharge.

Kreosote   The discharge is yellow, watery and acid, smells like fresh grains, worse after the period. There is an associated redness itching and smarting of the vulval area. There may be ulceration of the vulva and thigh area.

Borax   The discharge is like the white of an egg clear and copious, and feels hot, occuring in the middle of the cycle usually, painless with associated general anxiety and tension.

Pulsatilla   A thick milky discharge which is acrid and burning and excoriating, usually associated with chilliness and depressive tenderness. It is helpful in all forms of the disease.

Lumps in the Breast

Definition   A localized swelling of the breast tissue.

Causes   Cyst, abscess, gland, tumour.

Symptoms   Palpable breast swelling.

Treatment   *Conium; Phytolacca.* This problem must always be under medical supervision to exclude a surgical problem.

Conium   When there is pain associated usually worse before the period.

Phytolacca   Can also be applied locally as a tincture. For long standing cases.

Menorrhagia (Profuse Menstruation)

Definition   Excessive loss during the flow.

Causes   Hormonal imbalance, uterine displacement, fibroids, tumours, menopause.

Symptoms   Floodings, or the period is prolonged.

Treatment   *Sepia; Lachesis; Borax; Arsenicum; Sabina; Crocus Sat.; China.*

Sepia   Bearing-down pains in the lower abdomen, exhaustion, low backache, frequent outbursts of irritability, and depression is a feature.

Lachesis   Severe pains with the passage of clots usually associated with a very heavy flow or flooding. There is a most intense irritability and hot flushes are a feature.

Borax   Profuse discharge at night.

Arsenicum   Excessive flooding in the characteristic temperament.

Sabina   Especially in stout women.

Crocus Sat.   Painless profuse discharge (thin), clots, offensive, blackish, body cold.

China   Painless blackish haemorrhage.

Migraine

Definition	Periodic, usually one-sided headache.
Causes	Usually unknown, tension, allergy to cheese or chocolate, familial.
Symptoms	Headache, often settling behind one eye, nausea, photophobic.
Treatment	*Lycopodium; Natrum Mur.; Silicea; Sanguinaria; Pulsatilla; Spigelia; Thuja.*
Lycopodium	Headache is usually over the right eye. Nausea and dizziness are common. Pain is often worse in the afternoons and about 8.00 pm and aggravated by concentration.
Natrum Mur.	There is a throbbing, burning headache, often felt on the top of the head, worse in the mornings, aggravated by movement and from warmth.
Sanguinaria	Right-sided headache may be associated with pain in the shoulder area.
Pulsatilla	Right-sided headache, the symptoms are very variable and always worse from heat.
Silicea	Right-sided headache; the migraine begins at the back of the head to settle behind the right eye and right temple.
Spigelia	Left-sided headache, usually associated with weakness, fainting, palpitations.
Thuja	Left-sided headache, often worse after vaccination. The skin is oily and warts are common.

Nausea and Vomiting

Definition Wanting to vomit, and the actual regurgitation of the contents of the stomach and sometimes upper intestine with bile.

Causes Irritation of the stomach, psychological, may be deliberately induced, anorexia nervosa, pregnancy, Ménière's syndrome.

Symptoms Dizziness, retching, weakness and collapse with regurgitation of either undigested or partially digested food. Profuse salivation and sweating is a feature.

Treatment *Ipecacuanha; Arsenicum; Ant. Crud.; Apomorphia; Phosphorus.*

Ipecacuanha Severe nausea leading to vomiting after meals, the tongue is usually clean and perspiration is marked. The vomit is green or mucous.

Arsenicum There is a sensation of heat and burning, with an acid tasting vomiting after meals, nausea and general chilliness and exhaustion.

Ant. Crud. The tongue is coated white there is nausea and loss of appetite. Useful in children when the stomach is overladen, or there is excessive summer heat.

Apomorphia Sudden vomiting without warning, and nausea. Useful in alcoholics.

Phosphorus For vomiting associated with peptic ulceration, often of bright fresh blood. They usually desire cold drinks but vomit them as soon as they become warmed in the stomach. Burning pains are characteristic.

Peptic Ulcer

Definition   Ulceration of the mucosal lining of the stomach usually pylorus.

Causes   Stress, acidity, constitutional, familial, repressed emotion.

Symptoms   Pain, indigestion, flatulence, heartburn after meals.

Treatment   *Uranium Nit.; Kali. Bich.; Ornithogalum; Argent. Nit.; Arsenicum; Atropinum; Nux Vomica; Lycopodium; Anacardium.*

Anacardium   The pain usually occurs two hours after eating, with dull epigastric pain extending into the back. They are always better for eating.

Kali. Bich.   Nausea, vomiting and mucous formation with burning pains, usually worse after eating, in the stomach region.

Uranium Nit.   Gnawing pains, often in the afternoons or after food, acidity. Symptoms usually felt in the upper abdomen.

Ornithogalum   A very valuable remedy in peptic ulcers.

Argent. Nit.   When there is flatulence, gnawing pains in the pit of the stomach, worse with food, pressure. There is a craving for sweet foods which usually aggravates the condition, intolerance of heat, and a strong nervous phobic element strongly associated.

Arsenicum   Useful when there are severe burning pains and exhaustion, pain immediately after food, lack of appetite, often diarrhoea is present.

Atropinum   Severe mid-abdominal pains with associated nausea and vomiting, usually better for food.

Nux Vomica   The person is irritable, pains worse in the morning, and headache is common, better for vomiting, and worse after eating, pain occurs half an hour after food usually. Constipation is a feature.

Lycopodium   There is flatulence, pain immediately after food, the least food causes a sensation of fullness, a longing for sweet foods, and distress, should a meal be delayed or missed.

Phlebitis

Definition   Inflammation of the venous channels anywhere in the body.

Causes   Trauma, debility, smoking, the pill, certain hormonal preparations and anti-depressants.

Symptoms   Leg oedema, pain, redness, tenderness, incapacity.

Treatment   *Hamamelis* tincture locally; *Hamamelis; Pulsatilla; Arnica; Aconite; Lachesis; Belladonna.*

Hamamelis   The tincture applied locally and *Hamamelis* given internally in 6c potency. There are usually associated varicose veins.

Pulsatilla   When there are associated varicose veins and the patient is thirstless and intolerant of heat.

Arnica   The tincture applied locally and *Arnica* given internally in the 6c potency when associated with trauma.

Aconite   When the problem is acute and associated with fatigue as from long periods of walking and exhaustion.

Lachesis   When the area is bluish.

Belladonna   Indicated when the overlying area is hot, red, tender and infected.

Piles

Definition	Haemorrhoids of the anal vessels.
Causes	Pregnancy, perhaps with added constipation.
Symptoms	Pain, itching, discomfort, bleeding, prolapse of the piles.
Treatment	*Nux Vomica; Collinsonia; Aesculus; Pulsatilla; Aloes; Sulphur.*
Nux Vomica	When there is associated indigestion, waking at night from midnight to 2.00 am. Irritability and constipation is common. The piles are large, burning and stinging, often with a bruised low back pain.
Collinsonia	The most valuable remedy when piles and itching are very marked. There is a feeling of 'sticks' in the rectum, and usually constipation. They bleed constantly.
Aesculus	The rectum has a feeling of splinters. The piles are purple and there is severe rectal and back pain, with dryness, itching and burning in the area.
Pulsatilla	A very useful remedy in pregnancy. Often there is an associated indigestion, absence of thirst, and the piles bleed easily.
Aloes	Helpful when the piles protrude like a bunch of grapes, bleeding frequently and better for the application of cold water. Diarrhoea is common, and the anus and rectum have a scraped burning sensation.
Sulphur	Often very helpful when the piles are not bleeding, but there is constipation and anal itching. Fullness and throbbing headache is characteristic.

Pregnancy Problems

Anaemia

Definition   Low blood haemoglobin because of pregnancy.

Causes   Inadequate rest and diet.

Symptoms   Fatigue, lack of interest and energy, depression, breathlessness.

Treatment   *Calc. Phos. 3x; Ferr. Phos. 3x; Ferrum Met.*

Calc. Phos. 3x and *Ferr. Phos. 3x*   This combination taken twice daily is most recommended for the common iron deficiency anaemia of pregnancy.

Ferrum Met.   Is useful when the anaemia is more severe and associated with pallor and flushed cheeks, weakness and breathlessness. The 6 potency should be used.

Breast Abscess

Definition   An acute infection of the breast tissues, during breast feeding.

Causes   Usually unknown, or due to lack of hygiene.

Symptoms   Pain, redness, swelling, absence of flow of milk, fever, general malaise, axillary glandular involvement.

Treatment   *Phytolacca* tincture locally; *Phytolacca; Bryonia; Belladonna; Aconite.*

Phytolacca   Tincture externally, and *Phytolacca* internally.

Bryonia   When the breast is very hard and tense.

Belladonna   When the breast is hot, hard and inflamed, usually with a raised body temperature.

Aconite   For the early acute cases, with severe pain, restlessness, often high fever. Useful, particularly for the very acute abscess of lactation.

Breast Feeding (Excess of Milk)

Definition	An excessive accumulation of milk in the lactating breast.
Causes	Over production, or the child's intake and sucking is inadequate.
Symptoms	The breasts are heavy, painful and over-flowing.
Treatment	*Nat. Sulph.; Pulsatilla; Borax; Calc. Carb.; Phytolacca.*
Nat. Sulph.	Useful particularly during the first early morning feed time. The condition tends to come and go. There is always great sensitivity to cold and to damp.
Pulsatilla	The breasts are tense, swollen and painful. Emotional, particularly profuse weeping is a feature, and there is intolerance of any form of heat.
Borax	The breasts overflow between the feeds.
Calc. Carb.	As for *Borax* but in the *Calcarea* type of constitution.
Phytolacca	The breasts are very sensitive and there is an excessive flow of milk.

Breast Feeding (Insufficient Milk)

Definition	Inadequate milk flow during lactation for the needs of the baby.
Causes	Constitutional, or a shock, chill, poor sucking.
Symptoms	The child fails to gain weight satisfactorily, is frequently hungry, irritable and crying.
Treatment	*Chamomilla; Aconite; Agnus Castus; Asafoetida; Natrum Mur.; Sabal Serr.*
Chamomilla	The milk decreases due to anger.
Aconite	The milk decreases due to fear or shock.
Agnus Castus	No milk appears within twenty-four hours of delivery.
Asafoetida	The milk flows and then suddenly stops.
Natrum Mur.	The decrease is associated with grief or an acute emotional stress.
Sabal Serr.	When the breasts are insufficiently developed.

Breasts Painful

Definition	The breasts are painful, heavy and sore during pregnancy.
Causes	The most usual cause is from hormonal imbalance, affecting the glandular tissues of the breasts. It is closely related to the menstrual cycle, and often worse just before the onset of the flow.
Symptoms	Pain and discomfort.
Treatment	*Belladonna; Bryonia; Pulsatilla.*
Belladonna	The breasts are painful, heavy and red with a sensation of heat.
Bryonia	The breasts are heavy and painful but without redness and inflammation.
Pulsatilla	A useful general remedy when the breasts are swollen and painful either in pregnancy or after it.

Delayed Labour

Definition	The final stage of expulsion of the foetus, or dilation of the *os uteri*, is delayed, or absent.
Causes	Uterine inertia, head not engaged, breech, or transverse lie.
Symptoms	Weakness, exhaustion.
Treatment	*Pulsatilla; Gelsemium; Belladonna; Chamomilla.* A physician must be in attendance directing the treatment.
Pulsatilla	The contractions are mainly weak and irregular, lacking vigour. Nausea is often present.
Gelsemium	The *os uteri* does not dilate up and is rigid.
Belladonna	The *os uteri* does not dilate, there is headache, restlessness and flushed face.
Chamomilla	When pain is unbearable.

Delivery

Definition   The stage of explusion of the infant.

Symptoms   Pain, contraction, bearing down pains.

Treatment   *Caulophyllum.*

Caulophyllum   This is given in the last three months of pregnancy to ensure a smooth delivery and to avoid complications where possible. The remedy acts as a tonic to the uterine muscles.

Discomfort due to Foetal Movements

Definition   Awareness of foetal movements, with discomfort.

Causes   An over-active foetus, or over-sensitive mother, the foetal position may be breach or transverse.

Symptoms   Malaise and discomfort.

Treatment   *Opium; Arnica; Pulsatilla; Hamamelis.*

Opium   Usually when there is associated fatigue and constipation.

Arnica   There is a bruised sensation and fatigue.

Pulsatilla   Helpful when the uterus and the abdominal wall are sore.

Hamamelis   Another valuable remedy for soreness of the abdominal wall.

Insomnia

Definition	Failure to sleep during pregnancy, and to establish a regular pattern.
Causes	Discomfort of the pregnancy, the foetus is over-active, tension, fatigue, excessive coffee drinking.
Symptoms	Not getting off to sleep, or waking after a time and staying awake.
Treatment	*Coffea; Lycopodium; Sulphur; Aconite; Chamomilla; Pulsatilla.*
Coffea	Especially when associated with abuse of coffee or tea, and if there is mental excitement.
Lycopodium	Valuable when unable to get off to sleep due to an over-active mind.
Sulphur	When there is waking or restlessness in the early hours, between 2.00 and 5.00 am.
Aconite	If there is associated chill, temperature, or rigors.
Chamomilla	When there is insomnia due to pain or cramps and with associated irritability.
Pulsatilla	Of value in pregnancy when the person wakes about 2.00 am, gets up, or wants a drink and a biscuit, and only then falls asleep again.

Labour Problems

Definition   The labour is difficult and prolonged.

Causes   Abnormal presentation of the head, pelvis is flat, or abnormal, large foetus.

Symptoms   Prolonged and painful labour.

Treatment   *Arnica; Chamomilla; Coffea; Gelsemium.*
                   This must always be directed by a physician.

Arnica   When there is excessive fatigue and exhaustion.

Chamomilla   For a painful and difficult delivery.

Coffea   As above.

Gelsemium   As above.

Mastitis

Definition	Infection of the breast tissue during lactation.
Causes	Infection, usually local from the nipple, or accumulated milk, causing blockage of the duct.
Symptoms	Pain, fever, swelling.
Treatment	*Aconite; Bryonia; Belladonna; Merc. Sol.; Hepar Sulph.; Phytolacca; Sulphur; Silicea; Cimicifuga.*
Aconite	In the very early acute stages.
Bryonia	When the whole breast is hard and painful and tense with stitching pains; often with headache.
Belladonna	When the breast is hot with streaks radiating red, pulsating pains, worse for touch, movement or jar.
Merc. Sol.	When there is danger of abscess formation.
Hepar Sulph.	When abscess has developed.
Phytolacca	When there is hardening. Also apply the tincture locally. The patient is chilly, shivery and often with split or sore nipples.
Sulphur	When the pain is burning and usually associated with overlying skin disease.
Silicea	When there is chronic mastitis, often discharging. Helps break down hard lumps.
Cimicifuga	Especially on the left side, with pain, swelling, and hardening; often associated uterine troubles.

Miscarriage

Definition The spontaneous and premature termination of pregnancy, usually in the early weeks.

Causes Often unknown, or from acute shock, an emotional cause, hormonal imbalance, or from infection. There may be an abnormality of the developing foetus, or of the uterus.

Symptoms Haemorrhage, regular uterine contractions, abdominal pains, collapse.

Treatment *Pulsatilla; China.* Seek immediate medical help and hospitalization.

Pulsatilla When the placenta is retained after the miscarriage.

China If there is weakness from loss of blood.

Miscarriage (Prevention of Recurrence)

Definition	There is a history of miscarriage in earlier pregnancy, or of haemorrhage during the pregnancy.
Causes	Often obscure, but probably due to either hormonal imbalance, or an abnormality in the functioning and position of the uterus.
Symptoms	A recurrent tendency to miscarriage in each pregnancy, often at the same period of foetal development.
Treatment	*Apis; Sabina; Secale; Phosphorus; Merc. Cor.; Cimicifuga; Caulophyllum; Sepia.*
Apis	Useful in the third month. Bleeding bright red with clots, and dragging down pain in lower back and pubic region.
Sabina	Same as *Apis.*
Secale	Very useful in early months associated with frequent pains, pallor, air hunger and dark black haemorrhage.
Phosphorus	When due to disease of the placenta.
Merc. Cor.	When due to foetal abnormality.
Cimicifuga	A very useful preventative remedy when there are flitting colicky pains across the abdomen, which double-up the patient. Useful when there is a rheumatic disposition.
Caulophyllum	Very valuable preventative remedy with severe pains in the back and sides and abdomen, weak contractions and a scanty loss.
Sepia	An invaluable basic remedy, when associated with irritability, dragging down weight sensation in the rectum and lower abdomen with constipation.

Miscarriage (Threatened)

Definition   Bleeding or contractions, occurring in early pregnancy before term.

Causes   Often unknown, emotional, traumatic.

Symptoms   Bleeding, perhaps contractions.

Treatment   *Secale; Arnica; Chamomilla; Viburnum Op.; Sabina; Belladonna; Cinnamomum.*

Secale   When miscarriage is threatened during the early months, pains are cramping and premature labour is likely.

Arnica   When premature labour is threatened and associated with an injury or trauma.

Chamomilla   When associated with excessive nervous excitement.

Viburnum Op.   The threatened abortion is associated with spasmodic colicky pains around the lower abdomen radiating into the thighs.

Cinnamomum   When due to a strain or fall with slight pain but considerable haemorrhage.

Belladonna   When there is profuse hot haemorrhage, backache and headache aching and worse with the least jar or movement.

Sabina   Indicated when the threat occurs at about the twelfth week of development.

Morning Sickness

Definition	Nausea and vomiting usually in the early weeks of pregnancy.
Causes	Often psychological.
Symptoms	Persistent early morning nausea and vomiting during the first three months of pregnancy.
Treatment	*Ipecacuanha; Anacardium; Cerium Ox.; Natrum Phos.; Carbolic Acid; Kreosotum; Sepia; Aletris Farinosa; Symphoricarpus; Nux Vomica.*
Nux Vomica	Useful in morning sickness when retching and nausea is the most predominating symptom and vomiting is not marked. Constipation is often present.
Anacardium	Helpful when taking food relieves the nausea.
Cerium Ox.	For difficult chronic cases with severe vomiting of partially digested food.
Natrum Phos.	Also very helpful in the early months. Nausea with a sour taste in the mouth. The vomit tastes sour. Ravenously hungry immediately after vomiting.
Carbolic Acid	Indicated when irritability and headache is associated.
Kreosotum	Has proved of value in relieving the symptoms; nausea, profuse salivation, vomiting of water and slimy mucus. Better for warmth.
Sepia	The nausea is accompanied by a most unpleasant bitter taste. Bile is vomited. Exhaustion, straining, backache, irritability, constipation.
Aletris Farinosa	For difficult obstinate cases where exhaustion, fatigue, with fainting and dizziness are a marked feature.
Symphoricarpus	Of great value when the nausea and vomiting is very severe — there is an aversion to all food and generally the nausea is less for lying down on the back.

Palpitations

Definition   An awareness of the heart actions, often with a sense of anxiety.

Causes   Weakness, fatigue, anaemia, tension, hypersensitivity.

Symptoms   Consciousness of the heart beating.

Treatment   *Spigelia; Digitalis; Nux Vomica.*

Spigelia   This is the treatment of choice and usually cures the condition.

Digitalis   Helpful when *Spigelia* does not completely relieve the symptoms.

Nux Vomica   When there is associated indigestion, constipation and irritability.

Retained Placenta

Definition	Failure to expel the placenta (afterbirth).
Causes	Weakness and exhaustion, abnormalities of the placenta.
Symptoms	The third stage of labour, namely the normal expulsion of the placenta shortly after birth, fails to occur.
Treatment	*Pulsatilla; Secale.*
Pulsatilla	The placenta is not expelled after an hour.
Secale	Give every fifteen minutes. Usually the labour has been protracted and exhausting, with labour pains weak. The normal final expulsive labour pains fail to occur, and instead there is a twitching.

Sore Nipples

Definition   Painful nipples, and lactation is painful.

Causes   Cracking, inflammation, cyst.

Symptoms   Soreness and pain during and after feeding.

Treatment   *Arnica* tincture locally; *Hydrastis; Calendula* tincture locally; *Phellandrium; Croton Tig.*

Arnica   Apply the tincture locally if the nipple feels bruised and swollen. Not to be applied if the skin is broken.

Calendula   Apply tincture locally. Very useful if the skin is broken.

Hydrastis   The surrounding breast area is dry and burning, with stabbing pains experienced during breast feeding.

Phellandrium   When breast feeding is painful.

Croton Tig.   Severe pain is associated in the nipple when feeding.

Vaginal Discharge

Definition   A clear white vaginal discharge during pregnancy.

Causes   Infection, local irritation, thrush, leucorrhoea.

Symptoms   Irritation from the discharge.

Treatment   *Sepia; Calcarea; China; Platina.*

Sepia   A yellowish-green discharge.

Calcarea   The discharge is milky white.

China   When there is associated weakness.

Platina   The discharge is watery and itching is marked. Constipation and depression are commonly associated.

Premature Ejaculation

Definition   Too rapid and precipitate ejaculation by the male during sexual intercourse.

Causes   Psychological, usually in over-anxious tense personality, tending to be precipitate and hasty in most things.

Symptoms   Ejaculation is uncontrollable during coitus, and penetration is often impossible.

Treatment   *Lycopodium; Nux Vomica.*

Lycopodium   This is usually the most helpful remedy especially when the *Lycopodium* mental and physical characteristics are marked.

Nux Vomica   When there is rage, irritability, intolerance of imperfection in self and others and too many business or other worries which are not usually either delegated or shared.

Psoriasis

Definition   A non-infective chronic skin condition, characterized by dry, scaly, red and flaking areas, without vesicle formation, often in flexure areas elbows knees and wrists.

Causes   Unknown. There is often a hereditary tendency.

Symptoms   There is a chronic, thick and raised red circular rash in several areas of the body which irritates and tends to flake, crack or bleed. Infection and swelling of the surrounding areas may occur.

Treatment   *Sulphur; Psorinum; Petroleum; Arsenicum.*

Sulphur   One of the best remedies. There is a characteristic aggravation from water.

Psorinum   When there is a lot of irritation and scratching, even bleeding, scaling or dirty looking skin.

Petroleum   For use in chronic cases, when there are deep fissures and very thick, rough, dirty-looking, scaly patches.

Arsenicum   For the most chronic cases which are intractable. The skin is thickened and there is a burning itching.

Renal Colic

Definition   Severe spasms of colic in the area of the kidneys.

Causes   Renal calculus being passed.

Symptoms   Severe pain, doubling over, collapse.

Treatment   *Berberis; Calc. Carb.; Mag. Phos.; Ocimum Canum; Stigmata* tincture; *Dioscorea* tincture; *Thlaspi Bursa Pastoris* tincture. The patient should be in bed and given a hot water bottle to apply locally.

Berberis   Ten drops every fifteen minutes (of the tincture).

Calc. Carb.   30 potency, every fifteen minutes. Severe cramping pains, vomiting. Improved by the local application of heat.

Mag. Phos.   An excellent remedy for the severe colic.

Ocimum Canum   The patient writhes in agony, is restless and may pass blood in the urine.

Dioscorea tincture Restless, writhing cramping pains.

Thlaspi Bursa
   Pastoris tincture When there is a red or sandy urinary deposit.

Rheumatism

Definition   Inflammation of the sheaths of the muscles and the joints, with an acute painful often localized condition, sometimes with swelling.

Causes   Cold, damp, chill, draught.

Symptoms   Pain, often shifting or localized worse from motion usually.

Treatment   *Rhus Tox.; Bryonia; Rhododendron; Causticum; Pulsatilla; Ruta; Calc. Hypophos.*

Rhus Tox.   The most important single remedy. The symptoms are always better for heat and movement. The rheumatism may be in any part of the body — either large or small joints. Always worse for cold and damp.

Bryonia   The characteristics are in contrast to *Rhus Tox.*, and *Bryonia* has a rheumatism which is aggravated by motion and worse for heat.

Rhododendron   Is worse for a change of weather or an impending storm.

Causticum   Is a useful remedy, particularly when the jaw and neck areas are involved. Usually cases are better from warmth but not affected by movement. They are usually better for rain.

Pulsatilla   A very useful remedy in the *Pulsatilla* temperament.

Calc. Hypophos.   A most useful remedy for the sharp rheumatic pains of the wrists and hands.

Ruta   Useful in rheumatism of the knees and also the low back area and large joints.

Scanty Periods

Definition   The periods are regular, but the flow is weak, small and short-lasting.

Causes   Constitutional, adolescence, weakness, debility, pre-menopausal or menopausal.

Symptoms   The menstrual flow is small and weak and short-lasting.

Treatment   *Sepia; Natrum Mur.; Phosphorus; Pulsatilla; Calc. Carb.; Bryonia; Aconite.*

Sepia   Severe lower abdominal pain, associated with constipation, emotional withdrawal and solitude.

Natrum Mur.   The periods have never been established from the outset and always scanty and irregular. Nervous tension, immaturity, depression and lack of confidence is a feature.

Phosphorus   The onset of the periods was often premature and then ceased. For the tall, pale, thin girl, very bright and vivacious, but also nervous and demanding constant attention and reassurance.

Pulsatilla   When there is an absence of thirst in a weak pale constitution.

Calc. Carb.   In a flabby girl, when the scanty flow is due to anaemia or getting wet.

Bryonia   Dizziness, stitching lower abdominal pain and dry cough is common.

Aconite   When associated with sudden chill or shock, or getting cold.

Sciatica

Definition	Pain along the distribution of the sciatic nerve.
Causes	Traumatic, degenerative.
Symptoms	Pain from the mid-buttock, referred to the knee and ankle.
Treatment	*Colocynth; Carboneum Sulph.; Lachesis; Arsenicum; Gnaphalium; Ammonium Mur.; Nux Vomica; Rhus Tox.*
Colocynth	Usually right-sided, worse from cold, the pain radiates down the leg to the foot, and is paroxysmal, with numbness and weakness.
Carboneum Sulph.	Left-sided sciatica, usually from a chill, but paradoxically worse from local warmth. Stiffness is a feature and walking is often impaired.
Lachesis	Sciatica in either leg, worse at night and from cold air.
Arsenicum	The pain is intermittent, worse at night, better for gentle motion, but worse for cold and rapid movement.
Gnaphalium	For severe pain and numbness along the whole sciatic pathway, better for rest and sitting, worse from motion.
Ammonium Mur.	The pain is worse for sitting and better for walking and sleep. Often the pain is left-sided.
Nux Vomica	The sciatica is darting, shooting in character, the limbs are stiff, cold and feel paralyzed. Better for heat, constipation is common.
Rhus Tox.	When there is a chronic condition with burning tearing pains better for heat and movement, worse at rest, due to exposure to cold or damp.

Short-sightedness

Definition　　The inability to focus the vision, unless the object is brought excessively close to the eyeball.

Causes　　Often unknown, the fault is usually a weakness in the lens muscles which normally bring about focusing without strain or discomfort.

Symptoms　　Objects are blurred, out of focus, and increasingly, in order to be seen at all clearly, must be carried nearer and nearer to the pupil and lens.

Treatment　　*Physostigma.*

Physostigma　　A useful remedy in this problem. It is best given in the 3x potency, acting on the ciliary muscles of the lens. There is a peculiar dread of cold water in any form which is a specific indication for the remedy.

Stiff Neck

Definition	Stiffness in the neck region, due to rheumatism (muscular).
Causes	Draught, cold, chill, tension.
Symptoms	Stiffness, immobility in the area, discomfort.
Treatment	*Aconite; Causticum; Cimicifuga; Lachnanthes.*
Aconite	When the onset is acute, due to exposure to a cold and chilling draught. There is restlessness and anxiety.
Causticum	A useful remedy for rheumatism and stiffness, usually feels better for rain.
Cimicifuga	A further helpful remedy when there is severe pain, relieved by pressure.
Lachnanthes	For right-sided stiff necks, associated with sweating and pain in the upper arm and elbow.

Sun Stroke

Definition   Paralysis of all the functions of the brain, due to exposure to the direct heat of the sun.

Causes   Direct sun, physical exertion in heat.

Symptoms   Thirst, heat, collapse, vertigo, fainting, congestion of the eyes, convulsions may occur.

Treatment   *Belladonna; Glonoine; Natrum Carb.; Amyl Nitrate* tincture; *Gelsemium.*

Belladonna   There is a bounding full pulse, the face is red, flushed, and the eyes are dilated and bloodshot. There is usually an associated rise of temperature.

Glonoine   The face is pale, the eyes are fixed and there is vomiting, a bounding pulse, and heavy breathing. There is a severe pounding headache, high temperature and often loss of consciousness.

Natrum Carb.   For headaches and general ill-effects of the heat of the summer, particularly headaches and weakness.

Amyl Nitrate   tincture   When there is severe pounding headache, flushed face and convulsions are present.

Gelsemium   Irritability, dizziness, severe right-sided headache is a feature. Aggravation by light or movement.

Uterine Fibrous Tumours

Definition   A non-malignant swelling of the uterus, fibrous in type.

Causes   Unknown.

Symptoms   Swelling, discomfort, irregular menses and often a heavy
                   loss.

Treatment   *Sepia; Calc. Iodide; Lachesis; Aurum Mur.* The diagnosis
                   must be confirmed by the physician or surgeon.

Sepia   Useful in all uterine tumours, when associated with
                   bearing down pains and the *Sepia* make-up.

Calc. Iodide   This is one of the most useful and basic remedies to give.

Lachesis   Valuable to follow *Calc. Iodide.*

Aurum Mur.   One of the most valuable remedies in the treatment of
                   fibroids. It must be given over a prolonged period of
                   several months to be effective.

Urticaria

Definition   An acute skin condition, characterized by the eruption of wheals, often round, but may be irregular in shape, red like nettle-rash. Not contagious.

Causes   Usually unknown, often there is an allergic or emotional factor.

Symptoms   There is generally no other effect, than the appearance of the wheals, often in spring, or summer, with a burning tingling irritation.

Treatment   *Aconite* (if very acute and febrile); *Urtica Urens; Sulphur; Apis; Chloral Hydrate 3x.*

Aconite   For very severe acute allergic cases, with agitation, restlessness, anxiety and collapse.

Urtica Urens   A reliable basic remedy. There is a stinging itching irritation, with agitation. Both touch and water aggravate.

Sulphur   Chronic cases, with swelling, itching and redness. There may be ulceration and infection of the affected area.

Apis   The eruptions are swollen and stinging in character.

Chloral Hydrate 3x   If the above do not control, worse from the heat of the bed.

Varicose Veins

Definition   Swelling, irregularities, varicosities of the veins, usually of the legs, may also involve the anal area.

Causes   Pregnancy, the weight of the developing foetus, pressing down upon the venous return system, and causing stasis and back pressure.

Symptoms   There is an irregular swelling and tortuosity of the veins affected, with aching in the area, and sometimes an overlying eczema, with redness, itching, and irritation. The whole limb is often heavy and sometimes swollen.

Treatment   *Hamamelis* tincture locally; *Pulsatilla; Aconite; Silicea; Ac. Fluor; Carbo Veg;* Bran (to lessen constipation as a possible cause).

Hamamelis tincture   Apply locally, when acute.

Pulsatilla   When following childbirth.

Aconite   When due to fatigue and long periods of standing.

Silicea   When uncomplicated, often with associated infection somewhere in the body and cold damp extremities.

Ac. Fluor   For simple uncomplicated cases.

Carbo Veg.   When there is associated poor circulation.

Vomiting

Definition   Urgent regurgitation of the contents of the stomach, often forcefully.

Causes   Vary enormously, commonly due to excessive eating, dietary indiscretions, emotion, infectious diseases.

Symptoms   Nausea, sweating, weakness, loss of appetite, dizziness, faintness. May be clear, contain bile, blood, mucous, undigested food, large amount of fluid.

Treatment   *Ipecacuanha; Arsenicum; Kreosotum; Ant. Crud.; Zincum; Nux Vomica.*

Ipecacuanha   Simple, with nausea and diarrhoea.

Arsenicum   Prostration, vomiting, burning sensation in stomach, coldness of extremities.

Kreosotum   Chronic persistent vomiting.

Ant. Crud.   Nausea, foul white tongue, heaviness of stomach.

Zincum   Food is ejected suddenly, without retching.

Nux Vomica   The best remedy when the symptoms follow a period of dietary indiscretion.

4.

THE CHALLENGE
OF MIDDLE AGE

This is one of the most active and fruitful periods of life, often with a freedom from many of the acute financial pressures of the younger couple, and, for most people, more stability in the work field. Much of the urgency and the physical demands of earlier years has lessened, and this allows time to bring to fruition many of the hopes and ideas which were not possible earlier for reasons of insufficient time, money, and the pressing needs of the developing family. The home is usually more secure and a circle of friends established.

Although they are less dependent physically, at an emotional level, the children continue to need parental support for several more years. It is a time of achievement and success, a realization of plans and ambitions with opportunities to expand and develop in a personal way, based on experience, achievement and the inner status they bring. The couple are often still busy, but more out of choice and pleasure than from obligations, yet at the same time, middle age is a time of profound self-appraisal.

Having achieved certain ambitions, particularly the earlier material ones, there is frequently a sense of being somewhat trapped by the very things and events planned for over the years. There may be a feeling of flatness and disappointment, a sense of having achieved an external recognition and success that does not necessarily fulfil deeper and more subtle spiritual needs. These are less easy to define and are not always resolved by formal worship and churchgoing.

Others feel that they have not achieved the sense of closeness which they had hoped for in their earlier years, and the accumulation of all these feelings may lead to depression, a sense of wasted years and of time lost. All these may occur at the onset of physical decline, especially when there has been any neglect of physical exercise and of the body generally. Such feelings of self-appraisal and doubt are particularly common in the early forty year olds, although not always emerging as clear-cut cases of depression.

There may be outbursts of emotion, or problems of insomnia, with a general sense of being run down, increasingly prone to recurrent colds and having a lowered resistance. Often there are frequent visits to a doctor with vague trivial complaints that never seem to clear up. Recurrent low back pain is common and responds well to *Natrum Mur.* or *Sepia* which treat both the chronic pain and any underlying emotional features. Problems of acidity and indigestion are frequent perhaps leading to a peptic ulcer, and obesity is also common with futile attempts to diet. All these physical problems add to the sense of failure, defeat, and of youth and hopes being things of the past.

Alcoholism may occur as a flight from such self-doubts and add to the underlying depression and physical debility. Often such drinking and alcohol dependence has developed slowly over a period of several years. This is especially true of cases where *Nux Vomica* is helpful, typically associated with bouts of periodic depression and irritability, usually in the mornings.

At the same time there may be problems of marital stress. In men, perhaps an affair with a younger person in a search for the earlier hopes and aspirations of youth, although this in no way resolves the basic problem of adjustment to changes in the present. Women may be equally promiscuous, and have an affair, either in reality or fantasy. They frequently complain about the marriage, life in general, and how neglected they feel, totally denying their role and responsibility in these difficulties. *Sepia* is the classic remedy for such an unhappy dilemma.

In others such problems do not seem to occur, and there is a further period of intense activity, a continuation of the social whirl, full of planning and activity, with a rugged determination to stay ever-energetic and youthful. They become ageing Peter Pans, so that any crisis, depression or problem of self-appraisal is denied completely. With such activity-oriented people, it is the 'game' that matters rather than the players, and these players include the whole family and those around them.

Others feel that they have been deprived of life's chances, unable to achieve an ambition or position of status which for them symbolizes a success story. They feel depressed, and their favourite cliché is having 'missed the boat', being 'too old', or that it is 'too late'. Regretfully they complain that they should have worked harder, planned differently, or taken up some earlier opportunity when it arose. In a defeated way they believe they have missed their chances in some irreversible way and constantly bemoan their fate, claiming they can do nothing about it. There is a tendency to live in the past and to be resentful, often envious, of others who have been more fortunate. Generally there is a sense of failure and futility, which is just as negative as the more spiritual crisis of the self-made man.

Often these complaints hide a fear of making a change, or taking up an available opportunity such as a new job or more senior position, where there are both prospects and advancement. Frequently such opportunities have been available over a period of years and never taken up because of the conflict between the desire to stay put in a familiar, static situation, and the wish to make a move to achieve a long standing ambition. Such people are life's procrastinators, and inevitably this affects not only the person concerned, but those around them as the indecisions, regrets and complaints drag on without a possible end or solution in sight.

Tension and strain are common, often emerging as general fatigue and exhaustion. This tendency to remain sluggish and static shows itself in bowel symptoms, also with problems of chronic constipation and piles. *Nux Vomica* and *Bryonia* are important in relieving the general irritability and constipation of both mind and body. When prescribed in sufficiently high potency they can often help the person to reach a decision more easily and to overcome a chronic condition.

In others there is a tendency to rigidity and overwork, denying the need to wind down or make any change or adjustment, broadening their interests to prepare for an eventual retirement. With such people there may be an increase of work output at the cost of good health, common sense and well-being. When there is a problem of this nature, with marked rigidity of attitudes, *Arsenicum* lessens the tensions and gives relief.

Women often have difficulties with menopausal symptoms. Flooding may occur, or the flow be pale, fleeting and irregular. Sometimes the periods are missed altogether for several months, only to return with regularity for a further few weeks. Naturally such problems of hormonal imbalance and re-adjustment cause a great deal of emotional confusion, until either the periods cease altogether or there is a return to a normal rhythm.

Fibroids are also common causing abdominal swelling, often abnormally heavy periods and a weight-like dragging down sensation in the pelvic region. Remedies such as *Calc. Iod.* are often curative, and may permanently diminish the size of the fibroid. When the loss is uncontrollable, severe and heavy, surgery may be necessary but in many cases this is not required and there may be a rapid return to health in a few weeks. When anaemia is a complication, additional treatments may be necessary.

Sepia is a helpful remedy for many troublesome menopausal problems and is particularly valuable in cases of prolapse. *Lachesis* is another key remedy at this time for cramping pains, hot flushes and irritability. The common problem of hot flushes is also helped by *Pulsatilla*.

Men may experience menopausal symptoms of hot flushes, going through a similar psychological crisis to the woman. Because of the naturally strong links with home and family, serving as a psychological support, and also because many of the problems of women are expressed physically, as with the change, such psychological upheavals are frequently less severe than in the male. Some women may be psychologically disturbed, however, becoming tearful, hypochondriacal and fearful, translating any fleeting pain or symptom into a cancer or a heart attack. There is a common tendency to identify with a parent who may have died in middle age, recreating all the symptoms of that illness and re-living the loss, grief and mourning process. For such depressive disturbances, *Natrum Mur.*, or *Ignatia* are very helpful.

There may be a tendency to obesity and compulsive eating in a futile attempt to find comfort from underlying tensions. Such problems often aggravate any underlying depression and in addition may provoke gall bladder or digestive problems, and in some a rise in blood pressure. *Phytolacca Berry* taken in its mother tincture form is a useful treatment when combined with a calorie-controlled diet.

Interests and hobbies outside the work field are important at all ages, and particularly in the middle years. They are an important preparation for retirement and help in the prevention of disease. Interests are important for both men and women and most people develop them quite spontaneously over a period of years. Others, however, are less well prepared, with fewer interests. In such cases painting, learning a language, musical instrument or sport can be enjoyable, providing an outlet and source of contact with others.

All these stimulate and help prevent isolation, varying with the temperament and basic attitudes of the particular person. The essential is that they facilitate a sharing contact with others which is such an important part of healthy living. Many continue to plan an active sport all their lives, such as golf, squash or tennis, playing regularly throughout middle age, and retaining a high degree of fitness, energy and social contact. All of these help to counteract many of the frequent physical and psychological problems of this period.

There may be the added pleasure of grandchildren without the tensions and inexperience of the young couple, so that a more relaxed enjoyment is possible. Unfortunately, divorce or separation of at least one of the children is increasingly common, and there is often a physical need to return to live with the parents for a time while accommodation and psychological adjustments are made. This may cause a good deal of pressure and anxiety for the parents, particularly if they allow themselves to become over-involved with highly emotional issues. Often health and good sense are best served by remaining neutral and supportive, rather then becoming too carried away by the psychological stresses of the break-up.

The couple themselves are not totally immune from marital breakdown either. It is not uncommon for separation and divorce to occur at this age in a long-standing marriage where the basic problems and dissatisfactions have been buried and denied over the years. During this period of middle age re-appraisal, such problems are only then faced up to. Rather than continuing a marriage which is more of a pretence than a real sharing partnership, separation may be decided upon.

With ageing there is inevitably a tendency to be more vulnerable to disease, unless the general level of health is high and resistance built up over the years. Homoeopathy has an important role to play in boosting this general resistance, and freeing the vital protective energies of the body to maintain health. This is of particular importance when there is a low level of health as a result of physical stress or exhausting emotional problems. Prescribing the individual's constitutional remedy usually gives the best results.

Colds and coughs, winter bronchitis and flu are common in both men and women alike, and this is a period when blood pressure, angina and heart disease may occur. All these conditions are helped by well-chosen homoeopathic remedies. Digestive problems, such as constipation, flatulence, diverticulitis and gall-bladder troubles are common, particularly when there is a high degree of underlying stress together with a poor dietary intake.

Rheumatism and arthritis are usually mild in this age group although some cases may be severe and painful. Generally the response to homoeopathic treatments is positive unless the disease is exceptionally long-standing and severe. Alopecia is common in men, usually due to hereditary factors, but in both sexes it may also occur with stress and when the diet is poor and deficient in the essential B vitamins. There is a good response to the homoeopathic prescription of *Lycopodium* and *Vinca Minor.*

The seeds of illness have often been sown in earlier years when the treatment and prevention would have been much easier. Such factors as excessive smoking, the use of certain drugs, tranquillizers and sedatives over a prolonged period; stress and strain; overwork; lack of rest and exercise, all act to make treatment more drawn out and difficult.

With a harmonious relationship between the couple the majority of problems that arise are easily dealt with and are often no more than minor irritations. It is essential, however, that the level of health should be kept high, both physically and emotionally, and ideally some form of regular exercise such as swimming or walking should be continued throughout life. Some couples meet regularly for yoga or exercises at the local health club and find this enjoyable. The essential in exercise is always rhythm, regularity and enjoyment, avoiding strain and excess at all times.

Weight control is important in the maintenance of health, and where there is a tendency to obesity weight should be slowly reduced over a period of months to the ideal level for height and age. In general fats, particularly those of animal origin, are best avoided, or their intake kept low. Even when the weight is satisfactory the calorie intake should never be excessive. For most people, a light breakfast with added bran is recommended except when there is heavy manual work, in which case it can be more substantial.

Ideally some raw food should be eaten daily, either as salad or fresh fruit. Strong coffee and tea are stimulants and should be taken in moderation as they drain the reserves of the nervous system and cause agitation. Salt is best taken in moderation as, like all preservatives, it tends to firm and harden the cellular structures and lessens resilience. In the middle years it is not recommended to take more than the moderate amounts used in cooking. Salt is a significant factor in the causation of water retention and raised blood pressure, increasing the fluid volume in the circulation, and creating extra work and strain for the heart.

Such conditions as cataract are at least partly aggravated by the excessive intake of salt into the system over the years. Homoeopathic sodium chloride in the form of *Natrum Mur.*, is one of the best remedies for such problems and can be of enormous benefit. The avoidance of the excessive intake of salt is one of the best and simplest measures that can be taken to avoid heart trouble and circulatory problems in middle and later years.

Alcohol in the form of spirits is best avoided altogether by most people, although beer and wine are perfectly acceptable provided that they can be enjoyed in moderation. Apart from the odd social occasion, smoking has little to recommend it healthwise, and in this age group it is not recommended. The benefits of not smoking to health and energy levels are always considerable. Because of the dangers of heart and circulatory complications, smoking should be eliminated in any woman of this age group who is still taking the pill for whatever reason.

For most people, in spite of a lessening of financial and work pressures, the period of middle age is not the easiest to experience. Often they are disturbing, perplexing years, involving deep and personal changes in both body and mind. Physically there are profound adjustments to be made with a re-setting of all aspects of the physiological clock, involving changes at a circulatory, hormonal and energy level. Psychologically complicated changes also occur, at least as important as the physical ones, with fluctuations in mood, activity, libido and feelings. These disturbances may frequently emerge as bouts of depression and lassitude, or sometimes over-activity.

But this is essentially a period when all aspects of the self and relationships are put into question, and this inevitably includes the marital partnership. It is not surprising that such pressures easily cause illness or breakdown, and these may occur at a physical level as with a sudden heart attack, duodenal ulcer or raised blood pressure in a hitherto healthy person. In others there is a depressive breakdown, or a phobic state develops with agoraphobia, or sometimes quite a different but equally worrying problem as with a loss of faith. Homoeopathy can help to resolve many of these physiological disturbances — for example, the problems of hot flushes, migraines and palpitations. It can also assist the underlying psychological disturbance by opening the mind to more healthy perspectives and giving a calming pause for more balanced reflection.

SOME TYPICAL CASES

A man aged forty-eight came complaining of a painful and swollen salivary gland under his left jaw, which had been causing trouble over the past six months. The condition was intermittent, and had been diagnosed as due to an inflammatory blockage of the duct of the salivary gland by a stone. When seen, the gland was very large and tender. A second complaint was of bleeding from haemorrhoids, present over the past six years, operated upon two years previously, but returning unchanged after one year.

Although his general health was good, the level of energy was low, and he quickly tired. In general he was even-tempered, rather neat and tidy, preferring warm, bright and sunny days, but disliking the heat. All foods were enjoyed, particularly salt, butter, cream and honey.

Initially he was given *Baryta Carb.* in 10M potency together with *Hamamelis* in the sixth potency. Two weeks later he reported that the haemorrhoids had completely disappeared, there being no further bleeding or irritation. The salivary condition was unchanged, and the specific salivary nosode *Parotidinum* was prescribed followed by *Baryta Carb.* in the sixth potency, and later *Nux Vomica* and *Sulphur.* One month later the salivary gland condition had completely cleared and there were no further symptoms, leaving no trace of the swelling. Six months later there had been no recurrence of either the salivary gland condition or the haemorrhoids.

*   *   *

A married woman came, aged fifty-five, because of a measles-like rash over the upper chest area which had gradually appeared over the previous eight to ten days. The rash was bright red, irregular, and caused mild irritation. There had been no contact with any infectious disease, and the condition was diagnosed as an allergic eczema of uncertain origin. *Sulphur* was prescribed in high potency, in a single split dosage, and after four weeks the rash had completely cleared.

A further problem was a long history of hay fever, with marked sneezing, eye irritation and catarrh. The condition was always worsened by exposure to silver birch pollen, which was confirmed by skin allergy tests, and usually worse during the months of April and May. In March, *Kali. Carb.*, was given in the high 10M potency, and a supply of the specific silver birch pollen remedy obtained. The latter was not, however, needed because for the first time in many years, there were no attacks of sneezing or hay fever or of any other allergic problems, the patient remaining perfectly well and quite free of all symptoms.

*   *   *

A woman aged forty-eight came with her husband, having totally lost all confidence and with no interest in anything over the past six months. She was severely depressed, would wake crying and worrying, and had lost her appetite causing her to lose three-and-a-half stones in the period of the illness. She just did what she had to do at home and nothing more. Usually she was worse in the morning, and often woke around 4.30 am worrying. During this period there was considerable fall out and thinning of her hair, which was an added source of anxiety. She was very insecure on her own and clung to her husband.

All these problems had started soon after the marriage of their daughter, and since that time she had never felt really well. Often her mood was one of irritability, and at one point she had felt suicidal, but not in recent weeks.

Because of her terror of being alone, her dry skin, the loss of hair, and her marked sweet tooth, *Lycopodium* was given initially in the 10M potency. Two weeks later she reported feeling definitely better, with only two 'bad' days, and sleeping much improved. But when next seen in a further two weeks, she was again nervous, crying and in despair, waking at 5.00 am and feeling that she would never get better. *Kali. Carb.* was prescribed in high potency, particularly because of her marked dread of being alone.

A fortnight later, she was less irritable and not so exhausted, but still had no confidence with many 'bad' days, and crying a lot. Her periods were also irregular, having come on some ten days early. Also she complained of rheumatic pains in her right knee. *Pulsatilla* was prescribed and two weeks later she was better, had started work, and there was only moderate anxiety, with minimal crying. She was much more relaxed and, for the first time, smiling. The patient never looked back after that. She was seen twice more, with added confidence and well-being, and there had been no recurrence of her problem when seen six months after.

* * *

A man of fifty-four came, married for a second time for two-and-a-half years and trying since then without success to have a child. Tests showed that the wife had no abnormality, but that he had developed antibodies which were reducing the motility of his spermatozoa. During the first marriage, twenty-eight years earlier, he had had similar problems, and an abnormal sperm test at that time.

The cause of the problem seemed to go back to 1947 when he developed malaria in India, causing a massive infection of the scrotum. Because of underlying tension at work and concern about his problem, and also because of his very considerable intake of salt, as well as sweet food, *Natrum Mur.* was prescribed in high potency, followed by *Silicea* in the sixth strength. Two months later he developed low back pain and numbness along both legs, a recurrence of an old and chronic back problem. The spine was adjusted at the level of the third spinal vertebra by manipulation at the level of a displacement, and *Lycopodium* was given followed by *Silicea* as before.

Three months after being seen, a sperm profile was taken, and this showed a definite improvement on any earlier tests taken, with a motility better than the normal levels, and a sperm count and profile which was normal in every way.

*   *   *

A man aged fifty-three came complaining of severe difficulties with frequency of urination over the past two years. Investigations in hospitals had confirmed an enlarged prostate. On one occasion during this period he had developed acute retention of urine and needed admission to hospital and catheterization. Three months earlier the flow had stopped, and there was the threat of another similar episode. His work involved him in a great deal of travel, and high pressure, and he was often quite irritable and short-tempered. In general he disliked the heat, and preferred temperate climates. His taste in food was for rather fatty spicy foods, with a dislike of anything salty.

The stream of urine was often variable, weak and sometimes forced, with a tendency to dribbling at the end of flow. At night, he was obliged to get out of bed to urinate on four to five occasions, and this was exhausting him by interfering with sleep.

The patient was given *Sabal Serrulata* in high potency followed by the same remedy in the sixth potency. A month after, he reported a stronger stream, and that for several nights he had not had to get up at all. A further month after there was a definite overall improvement and he was less conscious of having a 'bladder' problem. Six weeks later the improvement was described as stable, and that he 'didn't think about it any more'. There was still some variability in the quality of the urine stream, but it was often very strong. Six months after this, improvement was maintained and the patient was discharged.

*   *   *

A man of fifty-three came with digestive problems, having been diagnosed on X-ray as having a duodenal ulcer a year earlier. The main complaint was of recurrent stomach pains, off and on, not related to meals but always worse for any stress or tension. These pains often woke him at 5.00 am, and had been present for at least the previous ten years. In general he was a quiet, easy-going man, usually good-tempered and rather tending to bottle-up any aggression, which inevitably occurred in his job, involving a frequent turn-over of staff. Generally he was too tolerant and too easy-going. Until his late teens, he had been a bed-wetter.

Initially he was given *Natrum Mur.*, followed by *Kali. Carb.* This led to some temporary improvement but there was soon a recurrence, and *Ornithogalum*, followed by *Nux Vomica*, was prescribed. After eight months of treatment, there was a complete relief of symptoms, with an absence of all pain or tenderness. His long-standing problem of haemorrhoids, which had caused considerable discomfort over the years, with itching and bleeding, also cleared completely during the treatment, without the need to give any specific measures for them. There was no recurrence of the digestive trouble when he was seen for a six-monthly check-up.

Flooding

Definition	Excessive and uncontrollable menstrual flow.
Causes	Menopause, fibroids.
Symptoms	Prolonged, heavy excessive flow.
Treatment	*Sepia; Lachesis; Ustilago; Platinum; Belladonna; Kreosotum; Bovista; Carbo Veg.; Crocus Sat.*

Sepia
Useful when there are associated bearing down pains and backache, better for violent quick movements better in the middle of the day and afternoon. The periods are often late and either scanty or very heavy. Sits cross-legged feeling that the womb will drop out.

Lachesis
The most important remedy usually controlling the condition. Headache flushing, cold extremities, tightness in the chest are commonly associated, also fatigue.

Ustilago
Another helpful remedy, giddiness is frequently associated, the haemorrhage is bright red and partly clotted. There is pain in the left ovarian region.

Platinum
Profuse with clots in a proud and elevated personality, full of self esteem, often depressed.

Belladonna
The periods are very profuse with painful cramps and bright red blood and there may be an offensive discharge.

Kreosotum
The period is early and very heavy, the abdomen feels bloated and often there is a dragging down back pain.

Bovista
A very useful remedy the periods are very heavy and occur every two weeks.

Carbo Veg.
Another valuable remedy particularly useful whenever the periods are too early and excessive.

Crocus Sat.
May be offensive and black, and the flooding is worse for any movement.

Heart Attacks

Definition   Acute insufficiency of the blood supply to the heart, by the coronary vessels.

Causes   Hypertension, atheroma, stress, anaemia.

Symptoms   Pain, collapse and shock.

Treatment   *Nux Vomica; Arsenicum; Cactus; Crataegus; Spigelia; Aconite; Lachesis; Digitalis.* This condition should always be under the supervision and direct care of a physician.

Nux Vomica   Indicated for the high-pressured, over-controlled, ambitious executive. Outwardly calm and suave, inwardly seething. Typically they have a short fuse and flare up with short-lived outbursts of rage, often in the home.

Arsenicum   Indicated for the thin, tense perfectionistic, obsessional work addict. Chilly, always over-anxious and fearful of the present and uncertain of the future. Generally unable to share and express their underlying fears and feelings.

Cactus   For angina pectoris, the chest feels tight and constricted as of a heavy weight pressing down and squeezing the chest walls. Worse for exercise.

Crataegus   This is a specific heart tonic, useful when there is shortness of breath on exertion and swelling of the ankles, usually indicating heart-failure.

Spigelia   Useful for palpitations, usually worse from motion and pain in the chest and back.

Aconite   Useful for the acute attack with severe pain worse for activity.

Lachesis   Useful in senile heart disease when the ankles are blue and swollen and the heart feels constricted by the size of the chest walls.

Digitalis   The most important basic remedy when there is collapse and a very slow weak pulse with anxiety. Worse for any motion.

Hot Flushes

Definition	The sudden experience of heat and often sweating, flowing over the whole body.
Causes	Menopause.
Symptoms	As above.
Treatment	*Pulsatilla; Glonoine; Amyl Nitrate; Strontia Carb.; Sanguinaria; Veratum Viride; Aconite.*
Pulsatilla	One of the best remedies and most useful generally in the *Pulsatilla* temperament. Always worse for heat, and thirstless.
Glonoine	There is the most intense congestion of the face and head with a marked throbbing sensation. Heat in any form aggravates the condition. The attacks are usually very sudden, violent, and unexpected.
Amyl Nitrate	Sudden overwhelming flushes of heat.
Strontia Carb.	There are sudden hot flushes, relieved by wrapping the head warmly.
Sanguinaria	This remedy has heavy profuse periods, headache and hot flushes, pain in the shoulder, especially right-sided is common.
Veratum Viride	One of the most useful remedies. Rapid congestion is one of the major indications for the remedy and it is of value where there are sudden overwhelming rushes of heat to the face and head.
Aconite	Helpful for sudden violent bursts of heat at the menopause.

Hypertension

Definition   Elevation of blood pressure, above the normal levels for the age.

Causes   Obesity, tension, strain.

Symptoms   May be symptom-free, or headache, fatigue, roaring in the ears.

Treatment   *Natrum Mur.; Glonoine; Crataegus; Gelsemium; Sulphur.* This should always be treated by a physician. Usually the weight should be controlled to reach normal levels, and salt intake restricted.

Natrum Mur.   One of the best basic remedies. Helps to relax the patient and reduces anxiety and eliminates any excessive fluid retention, reducing blood pressure.

Glonoine   Valuable when there are sudden pounding headaches and palpitations, a feeling of fullness in the chest, the breathing is often heavy.

Crataegus   This is a very useful cardiac tonic, when there is a breathlessness on exertion and an irregular pulse, often associated with heart disease.

Gelsemium   Useful when there is weakness, dizziness and fear of collapse.

Sulphur   Often proves very useful in difficult cases.

Indigestion

Definition	Failure to digest meals without discomfort in some form.
Causes	Dietary, peptic ulcer, infection.
Symptoms	Pain, flatulence, nausea, discomfort.
Treatment	*Nux Vomica; Natrum Mur.; Pulsatilla; Arsenicum; Lycopodium; Carbo Veg.; Calc. Carb.; Sulphur; Bryonia.*
Nux Vomica	There is heaviness after meals, heartburn, flatulence, and a bitter taste, always worse in the mornings, or after midnight. Nausea and vomiting are common. Irritability and constipation are a feature. Useful after excessive eating.
Natrum Mur.	Indigestion associated with nervous strain and tension, with heartburn and pain in the upper abdomen. Constipation. Excessive salt is taken.
Pulsatilla	Foods feels stuck under the sternum, the tongue is white coated, thirst is absent, symptoms periodic and variable. Cases crave rich food (starchy) which aggravate the condition and they are intolerant of fats. About two hours after food they feel full and blown out. Usually worse in the evenings.
Arsenicum	Dyspepsia, seen in a weak exhausted person, lacking appetite, chilly, unable to digest anything. Often with diarrhoea and of fastidious and fussy make-up.
Lycopodium	Craving for sweet things especially chocolate. Flatulence is marked and there are noisy rumblings and nausea, intolerance of any delay at mealtimes, causing an empty, all-gone sensation.
Carbo Veg.	Nausea with sour acid taste, wind and flatulence, pain in the upper abdominal epigastrium. All symptoms worse after food.
Calc. Carb.	There is a constant sour taste in the mouth. The appetite is variable and sluggish. Digestion is never good, tending to be noisy, slow and painful. Food is rarely truly enjoyed.

Sulphur	An excellent remedy for chronic dyspepsia with sour offensive eructions, constipation and flatulence, often useful when associated with excessive drinking.
Bryonia	There is weight-like pain immediately after food, nausea, a bitter taste and frontal headache. Pains radiate to the shoulders and back.

Lumbago

Definition	Pain in the low back, sacro-iliac region, involving the lumbar muscles and sacro ligaments in a girdle-like distribution.
Causes	Cold, wet, draught, strain provoking muscular rheumatism.
Symptoms	Pain, incapacity, worse for movement.
Treatment	*Rhus Tox.; Aconite; Arnica; Bryonia; Ant. Tart.; Sulphur; Cimicifuga.*
Rhus Tox.	The best remedy when due to muscular strain, after exposure to chill.
Aconite	In very acute early stages only.
Arnica	When associated with muscular strain and bruised type of pain.
Bryonia	For less acute lumbago, always worse on movement.
Ant. Tart.	Valuable when there is continuous pain, nausea and vomiting, worse when cold.
Sulphur	Helpful in chronic lumbago.

Menopause

Definition	The period of cessation of menstruation.
Causes	Psychological, end of the active reproductive cycle of ovulation.
Symptoms	Hot flushes, irregular or absent periods, emotional tension.
Treatment	*Lachesis; Pulsatilla; Cimicifuga; Veratum Viride; Caulophyllum; Amyl Nitrate; Sanguinara; Bellis Perennis.*
Lachesis	The most helpful of all remedies when the patient is always much worse after waking, with headache, hot flushes, sweating, vertigo and a feeling of tightness in the chest.
Pulsatilla	One of the best remedies for 'hot flushes' in a fair person of placid temperament who is very changeable and of a weeping disposition. Often with associated haemorrhoids or varicose veins.
Cimicifuga	Another useful remedy when there is irritability, restlessness and depression, with headache and a weak sinking feeling in the pit of the stomach.
Veratum Viride	Of great value in controlling troublesome flushes of heat at the menopause and after it.
Caulophyllum	Of help when there is nervous tension, emotional instability and excessive anxiety.
Amyl Nitrate	Another useful remedy for sudden bursts of heat in the head and face.
Sanguinara	For menopausal headaches and hot flushes.
Bellis Perennis	For exhaustion, backache, fatigue.

Menstrual Clots

Definition   The passing of clots in the menstrual flow.

Causes   Menopause.

Symptoms   As above.

Treatment   *Platinum; Ustilago; Crocus Sat.; Trillium.*

Platinum   The flow is early, profuse and with clots thick and black in the haughty, proud *Platina* make-up.

Ustilago   There is a bright red clotted flow.

Crocus Sat.   There is a heavy painless flow with black tar-like clots and abdominal pain.

Trillium   Scarlet clots are passed and painful knees associated.

Obesity

Definition Excessive body weight.

Causes Usually due to compulsive over-eating, often from an underlying emotional cause.

Symptoms Fatigue, slowness of response.

Treatment *Thyroid 3x; Natrum Mur.; Calcarea; Phytolacca Berry.*

Thyroid 3x Useful when there is sluggish make-up, a dry skin and falling hair, constipation often associated.

Natrum Mur. Useful when there is retention of fluid, contributing to the excessive weight. The remedy usually causes a profuse urination.

Calcarea In the pale bulky, flabby cold *Calcarea* make-up. Chilliness with most extreme feelings of weakness and apathy. Cases tend to crave eggs, and the appetite generally is capricious and sometimes bizarre. There is an underlying depression which makes any form of dieting more difficult because they tend to compensate by eating, particularly warm foods.

Phytolacca Berry Used daily as the mother tincture. This helps to substantially reduce the craving for constant snacks.

5.

THE ELDERLY AND THE DIFFICULTIES IN CARING FOR THEM

For many elderly people, ageing is a time of quiet readjustment of aims and values to changing times and patterns, even though the basic issues may not have changed much. It is a time of re-thinking, observing and cogitating — reaping the benefit of experience — seeing changes, yet recognizing patterns and sometimes mistakes of earlier times. The elderly often appreciate how such mistakes recur in the search for quick solutions to often seemingly insoluble chronic problems, where the only answer is a slow change of attitude, education and experience over a generation or two. There has been the time and opportunity to see such solutions and changes working in earlier situations, and time to appraise how effective they have been. All this gives a fullness, a wisdom and a philosophy which comes with years of experience.

There is usually a healthy attitude towards retirement when it has been well prepared for and accepted emotionally without regret. Retirement is a time of leisure and relaxation, and often a relief. Free from the pressure of work, there is at last time for a pause and a reassessment of aims and activities. With this feeling of relaxation and absence of acute pressure, comes the bonus of maturity as the competitive drives of the younger man lessen, and the libidinal dynamo finally runs down. The need to achieve can take second place to the more important priorities of the quality of life and caring.

However, with ageing, many old people become vulnerable and feel somewhat frightened and insecure outside the mainstream of society. This feeling is worsened if they are in any way resentful or critical of the inevitable changing and re-changing values and fashions which take place every few years. Many cheerfully accept a place on the sideline and enjoy the role of spectator where issues now involve them less directly. Others, particularly of the *Nux Vomica* temperament are still unable to unwind, relax and delegate, and continue to be intensely involved in whatever preoccupies them. They continue to play an unnecessarily active role, frequently putting intolerable pressures upon themselves and those around them. Because of deep-seated insecurities they still need position, status and prestige to reassure themselves of their intrinsic worth and value, and they do not fully profit from retirement and the liberty it brings. They repeat rigid behaviour patterns and are unable to change their basic attitudes. Often *Nux Vomica* in high potency, taken in the 200 strength, is helpful in breakdown down such attitudes of irritability and compulsion. It is frequently necessary to repeat the remedy several times in order to attain a degree of relaxation and stability.

Naturally, all these responses vary with the individual, and many people are exceptionally strong, reliable and alert both mentally and physically. They are able to work hard, regularly and efficiently, well into their seventies, often in a well-established profession or business situation. For them retirement is out of the question and would be unwise, as they enjoy to the full all the fruits of earlier hard work, foresight and planning. Such people remain well, and are often physically alert, fit and actively involved, dynamic, and interested in whatever is going on. They travel and remain at their peak apparently indefinitely.

With ageing comes the inevitable process of the body being less resilient, and the elderly may become less self-reliant and independent as physical processes decline, and vigour, strength and alertness of response become less reliable. This can be particularly seen with driving, when reflexes may have become blunted, and reactions are slower in any unfamiliar area or emergency situation. Homoeopathy plays an important part in overcoming such problems, and often gives an all-round improvement, with an increase in energy and openness of attitude as general health is improved by the remedies.

For most people there is a slow inevitable decline of physical stamina and a change in mental attitudes. A tendency to rigidity and repetition with less flexibility is especially common. When there is a hardening of both tissues and attitudes, *Natrum Mur.* and *Arsenicum* are helpful.

In every age group there is a need for reassurance. This is especially true for the elderly because of their sense of vulnerability. Depressive feelings quite often predominate, with a sense of loneliness and isolation. Such feelings naturally occur after the loss of a close member of the family, a friend or neighbour. *Ignatia* is the remedy of choice for these problems of grief and mourning. When there is the added problem of fear and lack of confidence, *Pulsatilla* or *Natrum Mur.* are indicated.

Such times are always made easier and less obvious when there is companionship and contact with other members of the family. The young couple have an important healing role to play, by paying attention to such commonsense psychology as stimulating interest and awareness. Regular visits can give elderly parents or grandparents something to share and look forward to. Talking, sharing ideas, discussing (without necessarily agreeing), and listening, all help to keep the elderly mind alert and supple.

At any age, when there is a basic lack of confidence, hypochrondriacal fears about death, cancer, or heart disease easily develop. In the elderly, such fears and preoccupations may be more severe and problematic than in other age groups. Any new physical complaint should always be discussed with the doctor to exclude the possibility of organic disease, and an examination may be needed. At the same time the doctor can explain how fear, from whatever cause, can create the illusion of sickness and so confuse the mind. Quite often, ordinary everyday complaints can become easily distorted into seeming catastrophes of nightmare proportions. Reassurance and regular examinations by the physician often help to keep such delusional convictions under control. When there is the utmost conviction of certain doom, whatever the reassurance and reality, then *Aconitum* in the 200th potency often brings comfort and rest.

Old people often feel lonely and become isolated by unfamiliar surroundings. When there is a move late in life, perhaps to a new flat or bungalow, it is not easy to make friends. Familiar faces and shops are missed, and loneliness becomes a problem. Stability of environment and surroundings always helps ensure security and confidence. A certain degree of confusion and disorientation is normal at any age when a change of home and environment occur. This can even happen when a much used room is rearranged or changed. Such feelings of confusion are usually fleeting and short-lived, particularly when the changes have been well planned and prepared for. A sudden, unplanned change of the familiar environment is a severe stress for an elderly person and may provoke the onset of an irreversible confusional state. There is a particular danger when such changes occur soon after a recent illness or operation or when there is an underlying tendency to panic and fear. For many elderly people, the ideal is to keep such changes to a minimum and a stable environment often ensures a gentle and happy ageing process. A thoughtful sensitive approach by the young couple can do much to prevent such problems of confusion and isolation developing.

When depression occurs, it is often a complication of a sense of ioslation or confusion. There has usually been physical neglect by friends and family leading to isolation, where the basic needs of contact, conversation, visits and friendship are missing. Homoeopathy can often relieve the depression and *Kali. Carb.* and *Lycopodium* are particularly helpful.

Insomnia is a common problem, sometimes aggravated by arthritic joint pains causing discomfort at night, often in the early hours. There may be a general sense of nervousness and inability to relax, especially after any change of routine, diet or established pattern. A combination of either *Lycopodium*, *Bryonia*, or *Kali. Carb.* usually cures the insomnia, also relieving the joint pains and any tendency to digestive upset.

Because of a decline in resistance and vitality, there is an increased vulnerability to all the problems of poor circulation. Cold extremities and a tendency to chilblains is common. Hypothermia, or a fall in body temperature due to cold, chill and exposure, may also occur and requires urgent hospitalization. *Carbo Veg.*, *Hamamelis* and *Agaricus* are important basic remedies in stimulating a more healthy blood supply to hands and feet.

Palpitations, fatigue and chest pains occur when the natural balance between the needs of the heart pump and its energy supply by the circulation is impaired. Often this is due to hardening of the arteries and is associated with raised blood pressure. A further complication is swelling of the ankles when the heart can no longer cope with its work load, and heart failure develops with breathlessness. Raised blood pressure puts an additional strain upon the body, and if severe and untreated may eventually lead to a stroke or cerebral haemorrhage. All these conditions need the careful attention of the patient's family doctor, and advice about diet, optimum body weight and rest are all essential to improve general health. *Crataegus*, *Natrum Mur.*, and *Digitalis* are remedies which help stimulate a return to improved cardiac functioning and better health.

Constipation is a common problem. The general sluggishness involves both the circulation and intestinal functioning. Usually this does not present a severe difficulty and *Nux Vomica* or *Bryonia* are curative. Attention to adequate daily exercise and the amount of vegetables and roughage (bran) taken in the diet is important in order to stimulate a return to normal bowel functioning.

The natural loss of elasticity in the tissues may provoke an increased tendency to uterine prolapse, and in these cases *Sepia* is often a valuable treatment. Piles and varicose veins are also common and respond well to the classical remedies.

Hiatus hernia may be a further source of pain and anxiety with a disagreeable burning sensation on bending down and on movement generally. The response to *Nux Vomica* is often very positive.

In men, prostate problems are a frequent source of discomfort and embarrassment. The response to *Sabal Serrulata* is often rapid and dramatic and can completely avoid the necessity for surgery. In both sexes there may be a tendency to bladder weakness which responds well to *Causticum*.

Arthritis is perhaps the major physical problem for this age group, and a common source of pain, discomfort and incapacity. The disease may involve the small joints of the hands and wrists or the larger knee and hip joints. There is stiffness and slowness, sometimes with wasting of the surrounding muscles, and weakness due to enforced inactivity brought on by pain on movement. Arthritis is frequently mild and more of a nuisance than a severe problem, although this varies greatly with the individual. Naturally the response to treatment varies with the patient's age, the severity and the duration of the disease. Usually the response to homoeopathic remedies is positive, often with increased movement in the affected joint. The major remedies are *Rhus Tox.*, *Pulsatilla*, *Bryonia*, *Ruta* and *Causticum*, according to the pattern of individual symptoms. Most arthritic pains are worsened by damp, but when *Ruta* is indicated as a remedy the arthritis is relieved by dampness and humidity, but aggravated by cool, dry air.

There is a common tendency for eyesight and hearing to be reduced over the years. Dizziness and ear noises (tinnitus) may occur with buzzing, humming and whistling noises, due to degenerative changes and impaired circulation in the middle ear. These problems are frequently helped by *Salicyclic Acid*, *China*, *Graphites* or *Rhus Tox.* Failing sight and deafness are often difficulties which easily lead to isolation and confusion if untreated. Homoeopathic remedies may give some relief although many cases also require additional physical treatments, for example spectacles or a hearing aid. Cataract is a common problem leading to misty vision and increasing blindness. In the early stages the process may be arrested and cured by the correct homoeopathic approach, while other neglected cases need ophthalmic surgery.

Shingles is due to an infection of the peripheral nerves by the chicken-pox virus. The typical blisters and scarring can be exceedingly painful for several weeks or longer. *Caladium*, *Rhus Tox.*, and *Urtica* help to speed a return to health. *Hypercal* cream applied locally is often soothing and calming to the area of irritation.

Much illness can be prevented by taking a few commonsense precautions. This includes making sure that the basic diet is adequate, nutritious and warm, particularly in winter because of the dangers of hypothermia. The food should be light and easily digestible, palatable, nicely presented, small in amount but not just a snack or out of a tin when alone. A good supply of fresh fruit is recommended according to taste, for vitamins, natural sugars and energy. Heavy meals and excesses are best avoided as the digestive system cannot cope with them. The main meal is best taken at midday rather than in the evening. For most elderly people, salt is best kept to a minimum, and spices and highly seasoned foods and fats are usually not well tolerated. Wine and alcohol in moderation, when part of a regular pattern, is enjoyable and in the evening conducive to sleep. Other than a small night-cap, spirits are best avoided.

Smoking is permissible in moderation, provided that it does not constitute a health risk aggravating bronchitis, emphysema or a heart condition. Whenever possible cigarettes should be smoked in sensible moderation — five to six a day being adequate for most people. However, there are no rigid or fast rules and many elderly people have smoked all their lives with no apparent ill effect. In a confirmed, habitual smoker it may be a source of considerable agitation and tension to try to eliminate the habit late in life. For the majority, the intake should be kept to a minimum, and stopped altogether should there be any signs of cough, wheezing or chest infection.

Clothes should be generally warm, light and well-fitting, as most elderly people are sensitive to the cold. They are usually fully aware of the number of layers which best suits their needs and comfort. Regular exercise, such as walks in the park or the country, a game of golf or a swim are all recommended, to invigorate and to maintain health, provided they are carried out within the limits of fatigue. This is especially helpful in the prevention of arthritis and stiffness.

It is wise to avoid putting undue strain on the spine and joints by carrying overladen shopping bags or using heavy lawn mowers. Particular care should be taken where there is a history of angina or any tendency to blood pressure. During hot and oppressive weather there is often an added strain for the circulation, and any extra effort should be avoided at such times.

A quiet nap after lunch is enjoyable and often necessary as reserves are at their lowest in the early afternoon. Most elderly people need less sleep and wake before other members of the family, therefore facilities for making an early morning drink are often appreciated as these early hours can seem long and tedious.

In general, health and activity are often only slowly diminished, although any sudden anxiety or change of routine can bring about a deterioration of vitality and health. There are no absolute rules for a long healthy life, but a happy marriage, a sense of humour and a philosophic temperament are important ingredients in maintaining youth and resilience. Hereditary factors may play a role in deciding how quickly memory and circulation decline, but feeling old is basically a mental attitude.

SOME TYPICAL CASES

A woman aged sixty-five came with a six-year problem of abnormal sensitivity to all forms of light, and could only, with the greatest difficulty, leave the house, wearing sunglasses at all times, and covering her head with a scarf. She was in a severely distressed condition when seen, with a dark red, swollen face, puffy eyelids, and any form of light or heat, caused the thickened skin to burn intolerably and to irritate. The condition had occurred at a time when she was using a steroid cream on her face for a mild eczema; she had dozed off in the sun, when in the garden, causing mild sunburn. Since that time, her face had been the cause of irritation, swelling up, and with burning pain at the least exposure to light, even the glow of a fire.

Pulsatilla was given initially in high potency, as her constitutional remedy, followed by *Cantharis*, because of the severe burnings in her face. Two months after an improvement had occurred, the face was not quite so red, and *Natrum Mur.* was prescribed followed by *Sulphur* and *Belladonna*. A month after, she was no better and very despondent and depressed. *Urtica* cream was given with a further supply of *Belladonna* in low sixth potency. Two weeks after this the skin improved again, became less red and sore, but worse for the slightest exposure to sunshine. *Sol 30* was prescribed, three doses weekly, and two months afterwards there was a marked improvement, and she was able to tolerate the glow from the fire, and generally felt a little better all round. But, still, the slightest draught, or sun's rays, was agony. *Arsenicum* was given in high potency, which caused a marked improvement. Four months after, she was so much better that she did not even flinch at the light, and the redness and thick swelling of her face had completely disappeared. There was no recurrence of the condition over the ensuing months.

*   *   *

A retired lecturer of sixty-eight came with problems of depression over the previous six years. Initially there had been a period of over-activity, quickly follows by a loss of interest and lethargy. All he wanted to do was lie in bed. His wife described him as a 'misery' and 'argumentative', with a poor memory which made him very forgetful. Over the years, numerous anti-depressant drugs had been tried without success.

Baryta Carb. in the 10M potency was prescribed initially, leading to an early improvement, in that he was not lying about the house so much, and was more active and positive. But, at the same time, he had become much more aggressive and argumentative towards his wife. The same remedy was continued without change, and three months after there was a more marked improvement with much more initiative and quicker movement.

When the rate of progress had slowed down some four months after, *Natrum Mur.* was given as he had stopped taking breakfast and was feeling miserable again. A month after, *Lycopodium* was given, which led to a further improvement in memory, sleep and activities.

At this point, for the first time, the patient could acknowledge an improvement and reported that he felt more of a person. After six months, *Baryta Carb.* was given, with further gains, and he no longer felt depressed, was calmer, and much more as he used to be before the over-activity six years earlier, which hd triggered-off the depressive illness.

*   *   *

A woman aged sixty-seven came with a five-year history of constant neck pains due to a 'trapped nerve'. She had worn a collar for several months three years earlier without getting relief, and was experiencing 'dagger'-like sharp pains on the least movement at the back of her head. These sharp pains were worse in the morning, at night, and on lying down.

The patient was given *Rhus Tox.* and two weeks after she was much better, more alive and full of energy, and the neck much less painful. A month after, she reported only very slight pains in the neck region and felt that she had almost forgotten she had them. There was a general feeling of being more positive, and the whining note had gone out of her voice, so that she looked, felt, and sounded like her old self. Three months later, there had been two occasions only of severe pain in the back of her head, otherwise she was very well. *Silicea* was given in low sixth potency, followed by *Rhus Tox.* A month after, she was well, and felt a different person, with all her energy back. Six months later there was no recurrence of symptoms.

A single woman aged seventy-six came with a painful, irritating shingles rash spreading round from her left breast to the back in the typical shingles line of blisters and infection. There was no history of contact with chicken-pox. Tender glands were present in the left armpit, and the rash was very hot, red and sore, with a painful black blistered area in the middle of the back at the level of the rash. Shooting pains and insomnia added to the distress. *Ranunculus Bulb.* in the 10M potency was given together with *Rhus Tox.* Two weeks later she was feeling better but still in a lot of pain. The shingles rash had improved, and *Rhus Tox.* was continued. After a further two weeks, she was still sore with some stabbing pains, but able to do more and the sense of restlessness had gone. Two weeks later, there was a much better feeling with no pain, the rash had faded and was healing well. However, she felt tired, and was given *Kali. Phos.*, followed by *Arnica* to help with the convalescence. The recovery was permanent without relapse.

★   ★   ★

A well-preserved woman of seventy-eight came because of recurrent falls in the street without warning over the previous fifteen years. During this period she had fallen nineteen times and had fractured her wrist on two occasions as a result of the falls. Her other problem was of cramps in the hands and legs, for many years, usually coming on in the daytime and always worse for any stress or strain. Another minor problem was mild arthritic stiffness in the hands and knees. She was given *Rhus Tox.* in high 10M potency, followed by *Cuprum Met.* in the sixth strength. Two months later she reported no falls, and that the cramp was mild. Because of her craving for salt, and a tendency to retain fluids, and for her eyes to run in wind, she was given *Natrum Mur.* folloowed by further *Cuprum,* as before. Two months later she again reported no further falls and that the cramps were much improved. Six months later she was well, and there had been a complete period of freedom from all signs of any tendency to falls or to cramps.

Aphasia (Post Stroke)

Definition   Inability to speak after a stroke.

Causes   Cerebral haemorrhage or thrombosis.

Symptoms   Sudden loss of the ability to articulate; or there may be confusion of words.

Treatment   *Chelidonium; Lycopodium; Arnica; Gelsemium; Kali. Brom.; Anacardium.*

Chelidonium   This is a very useful remedy, especially when there is associated deafness.

Lycopodium   Helpful when words can only be expressed with the greatest difficulty.

Arnica   Often helpful when the aphasia follows immediately after the acute stroke, and is helpful at an early stage of the condition in general.

Gelsemium   The tongue feels thick, paralyzed or slow and non-responsive to the mind and impulse to speak. Irritable, words come out wrongly.

Kali. Brom.   The patient is confused and fearful. Complete loss of memory, unintelligible, words are disjointed, wrongly used and out of place, agitated and very fearful of being left alone.

Anacardium   As if there were a plug blocking the mouth and tongue so that the speech will not come out correctly, and the tongue cannot function properly.

Arthritis

Definition	Degenerative changes in the joints, usually osteo-arthritic.
Causes	Degenerative or following a fall or accident.
Symptoms	Pain, incapacity and stiffness.
Treatment	*Rhus Tox.; Bryonia; Ruta; Calc. Hypophos.*
Rhus Tox.	The basic remedy of choice involving either the large single joints or small multiple joints of hands or feet. The characteristic feature is always an arthritis better for heat either local or general and worse for sitting and rest and on first rising. Movement which is sustained and continuous gives relief. There is often stiffness and aggravation on rising.
Bryonia	Useful for very painful joint conditions, worsened by the least movement or jar, but better for rest and cool applications. Like *Pulsatilla*, cases are intolerant of heat.
Ruta	A useful general remedy when there is relief from mild, warm, damp weather.
Calc. Hypophos.	Useful in arthritis and rheumatism of the hands.

Bunions

Definition	Enlargement of the bursa of the metatarsal joint of the great toe.
Causes	Usually due to pressure from narrow pointed shoes.
Symptoms	Pain, redness and swelling, with a permanent swelling and deformity after a time.
Treatment	*Hekla Lava; Agaricus; Silicea; Carbo Veg.; Nitric Acid.*
Hekla Lava	Useful in reducing the size of the swelling, and the main remedy to use.
Agaricus	When there is redness and irritation.
Silicea	Helpful when the skin is cracked and the extremities very cold and damp.
Carbo Veg.	Very helpful in improving the general limb circulation when it is a causative feature.
Nitric Acid	A remedy to use when the bunions become ulcerated.

Cataract

Definition	Opacity of the crystalline lens or its capsule.
Causes	Senility or trauma.
Symptoms	Hazy, misty vision, better in dimly lit conditions and looking indirectly and obliquely (there may be a halo effect). Worse in strong sunlight.
Treatment	*Calc. Fluor.; Calc. Phos.; Conium; Causticum; Natrum Mur.; Mag. Carb.; Santonine; Phosphorus; Fluoric Acid; Cineraria.*
Calc. Fluor.	Useful for any form of bony rigid hardness, particularly rigidness and toughening of the tissues of the eye.
Calc. Phos.	Where the vision is misty, diminished and blurred. Where any form of light irritates and causes pain.
Conium	Indicated in cataract when there is intolerance of light.
Causticum	Helpful in acute cases.
Natrum Mur.	Very helpful and valuable, particularly when there is a history of excessive salt intake.
Mag. Carb.	Useful when pain and spasm are associated.
Santonine	Indicated when objects look yellow.
Phosphorus	One of the most useful remedies, objects look red.
Fluoric Acid	The eyes are burning and painful and ache. There is the impression of grit or sand irritating the eye.
Cineraria	The tincture, one drop daily. For problems of lens opacities.

Confusional States

Definition   A state of cerebral confusion in the elderly.

Causes   Senile degenerative, infective when there is a high temp-
                     erature, toxic, organic disease of the brain, raised blood
                     pressure.

Symptoms   Mental confusion.

Treatment   *Opium; Baryta Carb.; Cannabis; Stramonium;*
                     Belladonna.

Opium   Useful in mild states of confusion, often with a red face,
                     headache, drowsiness and impending cerebral
                     catastrophe.

Baryta Carb.   For mild senile confusional states.

Cannabis   When there are flights of ideas, delusions and
                     confusional states.

Stramonium   Indicated if there is more violence associated with
                     confusion, restless running about and inability to rest.

Belladonna   Useful when the delusional state is associated with
                     infection and a flushed face, temperature and a bounding
                     pulse. Cases are usually restless.

Cramp (Nocturnal)

Definition   Sudden cramps, usually in the legs, at night.

Causes   Unknown.

Symptoms   The person wakes with acute cramping pains, often short-lasting.

Treatment   *Cuprum Arsenicum; Nux Vomica; Chamomilla.*

Cuprum Arsenicum   This is one of the best and most useful remedies — the cramps are often in the groin and abdomen as well as the legs.

Nux Vomica   Useful for cramps and spasms, usually worse at 2.00 to 3.00 am, and with associated irritability, constipation, indigestion, headache and nausea.

Chamomilla   Helpful when *Cuprum* fails in very acute and severe cases of pains in the thighs and legs.

Deafness

Definition	Loss of hearing in the elderly.
Causes	Degeneration.
Symptoms	Loss of certain notes and sounds, or may be complete loss. Often worse in a noisy room or when addressed indirectly.
Treatment	*Phosphorus; Pulsatilla; Graphites; Salicylic Acid; Chenopodium; Carbo Animalis; Iodine.*
Phosphorus	One of the most valuable remedies for problems of hearing in the elderly — often in a room when there are several sounds present, or the conversation is indirect.
Pulsatilla	Deafness, with roaring pains, worse at night and worse with heat. There is often a yellowish-green discharge from the ear.
Graphites	There is deafness better for movement in a car. An associated eczema behind the ear is common, which oozes a sticky honey-coloured discharge.
Salicyclic Acid	Useful in simple progressive deafness, often associated with Ménière's disease.
Chenopodium	The deafness is specifically to low tone notes and usually the auditory nerve is involved.
Carbo Animalis	Deafness where it is impossible to know from which direction the sounds come.
Iodine	Useful in temporary catarrhal deafness.

Dizziness

Definition The sensation of objects spinning around one, or a feeling of subjective rotation.

Causes Degeneration, Meniere's, post infective, confusion, emotional.

Symptoms The symptoms of vertigo, nausea, fainting, sweating, possibly deafness.

Treatment *China; Salicyclic Acid; Arnica; Bryonia; Theridion; Ruta; Causticum; Gelsemium; Baryta Carb.; Lycopodium; Silicea.*

China Dizziness associated with nausea, fainting, tinnitus. Meniere's disease. Worse from movement, draughts and cold air.

Salicyclic Acid Indicated when there is simple deafness, head noises and Meniere's disease.

Arnica Helpful in the early stage. Dizziness from sudden quick movements and postural change as from sitting up too rapidly. Mild nausea. Better for lying quietly in a darkened room.

Bryonia Useful in Meniere's disease — when vertigo occurs with any sudden movement as getting up from a chair.

Theridion When associated with nausea and is worse for movement.

Ruta When associated with eye weakness and strain.

Causticum Helpful in those cases associated with ear disease, and often urinary weakness.

Gelsemium Also useful in ear disease and when there is general muscular weakness and exhaustion.

Baryta Carb. When the cause is inadequate cerebral circulation.

Lycopodium Helpful in senile cases associated with poor cerebral circulation.

Silicea Useful in chronic cases when the general and peripheral circulation is poor.

Exhaustion

Definition   State of fatigue and collapse, weakness.

Causes   Physical or emotional stress to the body perhaps over a prolonged period, anaemia, convalescence.

Symptoms   Physical exhaustion and collapse.

Treatment   *Arsenicum; Carbo Veg.; Arnica; Opium.*

Arsenicum   Useful in a chilly person of fastidious make-up when there is prostration and collapse with thirst, and a dry skin.

Carbo Veg.   There is exhaustion and collapse but the skin is often cold and damp due to poor peripheral circulation.

Arnica   One of the most useful basic remedies. Stimulating the vital energies of the body. Generally it encourages rest, relaxation, and a sense of well-being and confidence. The depleted reserves can be more easily built up again and made available to the body.

Opium   When collapse is imminent and there is drowsiness and extreme inertia.

Eye Strain

Definition	Fatigue of the visual functions.
Causes	Ageing of the ocular muscles and the lens, working under poor lighting conditions and for too long.
Symptoms	Headache, lack of visual activity, tiredness, failure to focus correctly.
Treatment	*Ruta; Ledum; Calcarea; Natrum Mur.; Euphrasia; Gelsemium.*
Ruta	Useful when due to overwork. The eyes are hot and tired and painful, the vision blurred. Rheumatic pains are common, usually cases enjoy the rain.
Ledum	An eye tonic, useful for aches and fatigue. There is often an associated inflammation due to infection.
Calcarea	This is another very basic and useful remedy. The eyes ache and, like the rest of the body, feel cold and weak. There is irritation and a profuse watering of the eyes, better for warm eye-baths or compresses.
Natrum Mur.	Very useful when the eyes are weak, feel stiff and water easily. Usually cases take a lot of salt in their food, and are emotional.
Euphrasia	There is a blurred vision, worse for reading and writing. Pain, weakness of vision.
Gelsemium	Useful when there is eye strain with double vision, impaired vision and heavy eyelids. Squinting is common and associated with fatigue.

Failing Memory

Definition   Impairment of memory in the elderly.

Causes   Senile degenerative changes in the cells of the cerebral cortex.

Symptoms   Loss of memory for recent events in the elderly.

Treatment   *Lycopodium; Baryta Carb.*

Lycopodium   This is one of the best memory medicines. Loss of memory due mainly to extreme anxiety, and fussy agitation which is characteristic, worry about everything, fearing a future calamity, so much so that cases are quite unable to observe and concentrate.

Baryta Carb.   Useful in senile and pre-senile loss of memory for recent events in the elderly.

Frequency (Urinary)

Definition	The frequent passing of water, day or night.
Causes	Infection, diabetes, emotional, senility and bladder weakness, tumour, degenerative loss of bladder tone.
Symptoms	Frequency of urination, sometimes with urgency or pain. May occur day or night.
Treatment	*Cantharis; Berberis; Equisetum; Digitalis; Sabal Serr.; Nux Vomica.*
Cantharis	The remedy of choice whenever there is acute cystitis with burning pains, urgency, frequency and sometimes blood in the urine. Without the violent acute burning pains the remedy is not indicated.
Berberis	Frequency of urination, as the bladder feels imperfectly emptied, associated with cutting tearing pains in the kidney region, always worse on downward motion, as stooping, also lying or sitting down. Standing relieves the pain. The urine is slimey and reddish brown.
Equisetum	This is a useful remedy with frequency and less urgency and pain than *Cantharis*. The bladder feels constantly full and the urine is scanty and usually contains a lot of mucous. Nocturia is frequent.
Digitalis	There is an urgent desire to urinate often associated with prostatic enlargement and a dragging bladder pressure sensation is characteristic.
Sabal Serr.	Another useful remedy where the frequency is associated with prostatic enlargement.
Nux Vomica	There is frequency with burning pains but only small drops are passed. Straining is common and dribbling of urine a feature.

Incontinence

Definition   Loss of normal bladder control, associated with bed-wetting and incontinence.

Causes   Infection, senility, confusional state.

Symptoms   Bed-wetting day or night, or both.

Treatment   *Causticum; Ferrum Phos.; Baryta Carb.; Equisetum; Nux Vomica; Gelsemium; Sabal Serr.; Apis.*

Causticum   One of the most useful remedies, with dribbling; often involuntary loss when coughing or laughing, and general bladder weakness, with delayed starting and finishing.

Ferrum Phos.   When there is an inability to control the urine.

Baryta Carb.   When incontinence is due to senility.

Equisetum   When there is an associated infection.

Nux Vomica   Indicated when there is dribbling and loss of control. Often associated with tearing pain and irritability.

Gelsemium   Useful when the prostate is enlarged and there is a stone in the bladder.

Sabal Serr.   When associated with enlarged prostate.

Apis   Useful when little urine is passed, there is drowsiness and oedema of the extremities and a lack of thirst. Stinging burning pains are often associated.

Painful Joints (Hip)

Definition   Hip pain, usually arthritic in type.

Causes   Arthritis.

Symptoms   Pain and incapacity.

Treatment   *Rhus Tox.; Bryonia; Ruta.*

Rhus Tox.   The first remedy to give when there is stiffness and pain at rest, worse on rising and better for sustained movement and heat. Pains are always worse for cold and damp.

Bryonia   For arthritis when this condition is better for rest and worse for movement and heat.

Ruta   A useful remedy for arthritis and rheumatism of the hip and large joints — often better for rain when the temperature is mild.

Painful Joints (Knees)

Definition   Pain in the joint of the knee.

Causes   Arthritis, usually.

Symptoms   Pain and stiffness, incapacity.

Treatment   *Pulsatilla; Rhus Tox.; Bryonia; Ruta.*

Pulsatilla   This is one of the best remedies for knee arthritis. They are worse for heat and better for walking in cool weather. The *Pulsatilla* patient is thirstless and often chilly, but above all, the pains and symptoms are very variable. The knees crack a lot.

Rhus Tox.   Useful when the pains are improved by warmth and continued walking and movement; worse for cold, chill, draught and damp and for prolonged sitting. They are always stiff on rising.

Bryonia   For knee arthritis worse for heat, better for coolness and cool applications; better for rest; aggravated by any movement.

Ruta   A very valuable knee remedy where the sufferer is better for warm damp weather.

Poor Circulation

Definition	Poor peripheral circulation.
Causes	Arteriosclerosis.
Symptoms	Coldness, blueness, gangrene, chilblain.
Treatment	*Carbo Veg.; Lachesis; Pulsatilla.*
Carbo Veg.	This is one of the best remedies when blue, ice-cold, often perspiring, hands and feet.
Lachesis	Indicated when the extremities are very mauve or blue and less icy than with *Carbo Veg.*
Pulsatilla	Useful in the *Pulsatilla* make-up, when intolerant of heat and thirstless.

Ptosis of Eyelids

Definition	Weakness of the upper eyelids.
Causes	Fatigue, myasthenia gravis, oedema of the orbital area, stroke, cerebral thrombosis, Bell's palsy.
Symptoms	Drooping of the lid may obscure vision; loss of muscular power in the area.
Treatment	*Gelsemium.*
Gelsemium	Useful when there is weakness, often associated with double vision, giddiness and pain in the eyeball.

Retention of Urine

Definition	The inability to pass urine and empty the bladder.
Causes	Senility, post-operative.
Symptoms	Pain, abdominal distention.
Treatment	*Causticum; Nux Vomica; Opium; Stramonium; Camphor.*
Causticum	Useful in paralysis and retention of urine after operations. Usually the patient has had problems of delayed starting or in finishing the last few drops of the flow.
Nux Vomica	Associated with burning tearing pains, irritability, ineffective attempts to urinate, and an acute feeling of a full bladder. Often this follows an abuse of food or alcohol.
Opium	The bladder is full and paralyzed but the patient has no pain or awareness or desire to pass water.
Stramonium	The usually violent, excitable *Stramonium* patient passes no urine because none is secreted into the bladder.
Camphor	Valuable when there is a retention due to spasm.

Shingles

Definition	Infection of the elderly with the chicken-pox virus, forming large vesicles along the pathway of the nerve affected.
Causes	Infection with the specific virus.
Symptoms	The typical eruption of vesicles, pain, irritation, insomnia, followed by scars and, in some, neuralgia after the attack.
Treatment	*Rhus Tox.; Urtica; Apis; Arsenicum.*
Rhus Tox.	Useful when there is the local eruption with redness, itching, vesicle formation. Cases feel better for warmth and movement and worse in bed.
Urtica	Useful when there is more swelling and large vesicle formation.
Apis	There is burning, stinging pain with redness and swelling. The patient is thirstless and restless. Little urine is passed.
Arsenicum	Useful in acute cases with burning pains, restlessness and prostration. The pains are worse at night after midnight and anxiety is marked. The patient is chilly and usually better for local heat applications and warmth generally.

Stroke

Definition	Paralysis of parts of the body.
Causes	Cerebral haemorrhage, tumour, thrombosis.
Symptoms	Loss of power in the affected part of the body, complete or partial.
Treatment	*Opium; Guaiacum; Nux Vomica; Arnica; Phosphorus; Aconite; Baryta Carb.; Laurocerasus; Glonoine; Belladonna.* Treatment must be directed by a physician in the acute stages.
Opium	The patient is flushed, slow and collapsing, or unconscious. The face is flushed and dark, and breathing is heavy, the pulse is slow and pupils dilated. Useful to prevent a threatened attack.
Guaiacum	Weakness is marked, the limbs lack co-ordination and strength, often painful. Forgetful.
Nux Vomica	Spasms of irritability and confusion. The limbs are weak but there are often sudden spasms of jerky movements.
Arnica	A basic remedy. There is either an impending threatened stroke, or weakness of the left side. Bedsores are a feature, a full pulse and noisy laboured breathing.
Phosphorus	Depression, weakness and anxiety are marked features together with a feeling of apathy and exhaustion. Useful in degenerative or toxic conditions.
Aconite	Useful in the very eary stages particularly when there is marked anxiety. The skin is hot and dry and the pulse bounding.
Baryta Carb.	Useful for the period of paralysis after the acute episode, particularly if right-sided paralysis which involves the tongue.
Lauracerasus	In acute form of stroke, without warning, with collapse and a cold sweating skin.

Glonoine   Another useful remedy for a threatened attack with headache and fullness of the heart.

Belladonna   Indicated when there is unconsciousness, a red face, dilated pupils and loss of bladder control. Acute retention of urine may occur.

Tinnitus (Noises in the Ears)

Definition   The subjective impression of noises in the ears and head.

Symptoms   Various noises and sounds are heard in the head.

Causes   Senility, hypertensive, Meniere's disease, delusional, infective, tumour.

Treatment   *China; Causticum; Salicylic Acid; Sanguinaria; Lachesis; Aurum; Calc. Carb.; Ferrum Phos.; Carboneum Sulph.; Belladonna; Sulphur.*

China   This is one of the best remedies. Roaring, ringing, or tinkling in the ears, always worsened by movement.

Causticum   Roaring and buzzing sounds are heard and sounds generally re-echo.

Salicylic Acid   One of the most useful remedies, often associated with Meniere's disease. There is frequently pain in the cartilages of the ear.

Sanguinaria   There are roaring and humming noises in the ears and over-sensitivity to sounds generally. Rheumatic right shoulder pain is frequently associated.

Lachesis   Roaring singing sounds in the ears, catarrhal in type, better for shaking the ear with a finger.

Aurum   Has roaring in the ears and boring pains, associated with a severely depressive make-up.

Calc. Carb.   For chronic ear problems in the *Calcarea* make-up; the noises are humming and roaring.

Ferrum Phos.   Useful in anaemic patients when there is heat, ear-noises. Over-sensitive to noise, but no deafness associated.

Carbonium Sulph.   Ringing or buzzing noises, worse from walking or movement and heat.

Belladonna   Irritating and constant high-pitched ringing or humming noises. Agitation.

Sulphur   Humming or gurgling noises in the ears. Chronic infection, often with a pussy discharge.

Varicose Ulcer

Definition   Leg ulceration, due to varicose veins; usually poor circulation.

Causes   Varicose veins, poor circulation, often trauma.

Symptoms   Pain and the ulcer may be red and inflamed.

Treatment   *Carbo Veg.; Pulsatilla; Hypericum; Hamamelis; Merc. Sol.; Lachesis.*

Carbo Veg.   When there is weakness, coldness, collapse, and very poor peripheral circulation.

Pulsatilla   Useful in chronic cases with intolerance of heat and lack of thirst.

Hypericum   The tincture and ointment is very useful. Honey is another helpful local application.

Hamamelis   A very useful basic remedy. The circulation is poor and the limb is icy cold, the area surrounding the ulcer is deep bluish-red, sore and painful.

Merc. Sol.   When there is infection, pus and foul-smelling discharge.

Lachesis   When there is a mauve-blue colour of the area, often left-sided and chronic. Usually they are most painful on waking and any constriction of the body by tight clothing is poorly tolerated.

USEFUL ADDRESSES

Each of the following organizations was founded to promote the study and practice of homeopathy in the United States. These nonprofit groups, comprised of physicians, adjunct health care professionals, and lay people, provide beginning, intermediate, and advanced training in homeopathy to lay people and health professionals, publish monthly or quarterly newsletters, and provide many other valuable services and information to members.

American Nutritional Medical Association, Inc.
3366 Parade Circle Drive, East
Colorado Springs, CO 80917

International Foundation for Homeopathy
2236 Eastlake Avenue
Seattle, WA 98102
206-324-8230

National Center for Homeopathy
1500 Massachusetts Avenue, N.W.
Suite 41
Washington, DC 20005
202-223-6182

INDEX